THE SCHC ... GIRL

JOSEPHINE ELDER

Girls Gone By Publishers

COMPLETE AND UNABRIDGED

Published by

Girls Gone By Publishers
4 Rock Terrace, Coleford, Radstock, Somerset BA3 5NF

The Scholarship Girl first published by W and R Chambers, Limited, 1925
'Guide Isabella' and 'The Reformers' first published by Oxford University Press
This edition published 2011

Cover Design by Ken Websdale
Typeset in England by Little Pink Cloud Limited
Printed and bound by CPI Group (UK) Ltd, Croydon CR0 4YY

ISBN 978-1-84745-122-4

Francesca was sliding monkey-like downwards. (PAGE 61)

CONTENTS

INTRODUCTION

The Scholarship Girl was Josephine Elder's second full-length book and is a sequel to her first, *Erica Wins Through*, in the sense that it is set in the same school and features Erica and her friends as games captain and prefects. It is, however, very much Monica's story: Monica Baxter, from a National School in the East End (or eastern suburbs) of London, who has won an open scholarship to the prestigious Greystones School and is given the disastrous advice by her old teacher that she should devote herself to work and not waste any time on games. Any self-respecting school-story devotee could tell Monica that this is not a good idea, and so of course it proves. Monica rejects Erica's invitation to join in games, though in fact she enjoys hockey and hopes dismally that she won't be too old for games by the time she's won the right to take part by gaining a further scholarship that will take her on to college.

Luckily, Monica is rescued from her self-imposed narrow outlook by the arrival of Francesca Lucas, daughter of a Cambridge don, who has no hang-ups about Monica's impoverished background and is able to make her see that she needs a healthy body to contain a healthy mind. She teaches her, too, that she has to be part of the school, not merely out to gain her own advantage, and once Monica has starred on the hockey field (despite having given vent to a 'D—!') we know that she, too, is going to win through. Unusually for Elder, we have a small hint of Christian input, when the friends develop a devotion to St Francis of Assisi and decide to take his life as their model. Perhaps fortunately, this remains very much understated—possibly strict Franciscan ideals would not have gone down too well at a prestigious girls' boarding school.

The theme of the scholarship girl was, as we shall see, to be a popular one, and though Elder is not the first writer to deal with it she is among the first to use it as the main idea of a book. Earlier writers had concentrated on the idea of a scholarship or prize which must be won to keep a girl at school or take her on to college—Mrs Henry Clarke's *The Ravensworth Scholarship* (1894) is probably the earliest, but the theme had been taken over from the boys' school story (for example, *The Fifth Form at St Dominic's*, 1887). Dorothea Moore's *Greta of the Guides* (1922) may be the first to take a girl from a lower social sphere by means of a scholarship into a 'posh' girls' school, but, obviously, her emphasis in this book is on the sisterhood of all Guides. Elder used the same idea but placed it entirely in the context of school, though admittedly the Lucas family's Cambridge household plays a large part in Monica's assimilation of middle-class attitudes.

Elder's treatment of the subject, though praiseworthy in its portrayal of Monica's widening understanding, is in fact a little perfunctory in its handling of her social situation. Monica does not seem to have any difficulty in adapting to the middle-class habits expected of her at school—indeed, her very first run-in with authority comes when she takes an early bath before her dormitory prefect, and persists in doing so on a daily basis. Her only fault here turns out to have been the taking of a warm bath (and failure to open the window on leaving, though she does clean the bath after herself). Presumably, like the Chalet schoolgirls, her morning dip should have been cold or 'chill off'. But would a girl from her working-class background (her father is a plumber) really have taken a daily bath as a matter of course? Again, we are not shown that she has any difficulty over such matters as the names of meals—not, perhaps, to be expected at school, where the midday meal was no doubt 'dinner' rather than 'luncheon', but perhaps more likely to be a problem when she visits Francesca's cultured Cambridge home? Elder does show us Monica's initial selfish behaviour on the hockey field, together with her swearing, but she does not really get to grips with the different mindset which this behaviour suggests. There is reference, too, to Monica's Cockney accent, but not much is made of it.

What is really not terribly believable is the way most of the other girls at Greystones do not ostracise Monica because of her lowly origins. They are not particularly friendly, but they are not portrayed as despising her for her background. Only her odious dormitory prefect displays the kind of snobbishness we might expect, and she is shown to be considered at fault by the praiseworthy Erica and her circle.

There are some references, not many, to Monica's non-uniform clothes not being up to standard—her mackintosh has been bought to allow for growth and her dressing-gown and pyjamas are faded—but little is made of this surely very real potential for difficulty. (A more realistic treatment of the subject occurs in Irene Mossop's *Well Played, Juliana!*, discussed below.)

Another aspect of Monica's removal to a different world which Elder does not deal with at all is the probability that she would find it difficult, even if only in the first instance, to relate to her own family when she went back to them. This is a common enough problem with teenagers beginning to 'find themselves', but Monica continues to have a good relationship with her parents, while her brothers—and her former schoolfellows—are not mentioned at this point. There would surely, at least in the initial stages, have been a period when they might see her as 'stuck up' and she might be critical because they did not come up to her new standards.

But *The Scholarship Girl* is one of the first to tackle the theme seriously, and it is perhaps unreasonable to expect it to deal with all the aspects of it with equal competence. Elder was aiming to show the importance of a balanced life, and in this she succeeds. Like *Erica Wins Through*, *The Scholarship Girl* does not achieve the complexity of Elder's masterpiece, *Evelyn Finds Herself*, but it does show an advance on the earlier book and holds out the promise of what was to come. Monica is intrinsically a more sympathetic and interesting character than Erica, and we are made to care that she should succeed in rubbing off her corners. Elder could, and would, do better, but the book is by no means negligible and is an interesting treatment of a theme which many girls must have experienced in real life.

The theme of the scholarship girl is a favourite one with school-story writers, and many of the major authors dealt with it in one way or another. They were quick to see the narrative potential of a girl coming from a poor background and plunged into a more-or-less exclusive school, getting into difficulties with wealthier and often more snobbish schoolfellows but in the end making good by conforming to upper-middle-class mores. A version of the idea already existed in which a similar girl is rescued from poverty by a change of fortune—usually discovery by a long-lost relative or adoption by a wealthy godparent—but the scholarship girl refines the theme by having won her promotion through her own efforts. A scholarship girl, almost by definition, is noted for her brains, and can at least approach her new circumstances with the confidence that she is not in fact as worthless as some of her new companions think her and with the possibility of an interesting career ahead of her.

On the other hand, there is also the girl who has been awarded a scholarship or bursary through no particular merit of her own but as an object of charity. She is quite often the object of scorn, as in the early *Kitty O'Donovan* by L T Meade, where the Cupp girls are at school through the bounty of the headmistress. A considerably later example is Dorita Fairlie Bruce's Fern, in *The New House at Springdale* (1934), who is virtually blackmailed by her unpleasant schoolfellows because her fees are paid for her. She, like the other girls in this situation, although impoverished, is of the same social status as the rest of the school.

Elsie J Oxenham introduced a scholarship girl into *The Girls of the Hamlet Club* (1914): Miriam Honor is at Miss Macey's school on a scholarship, having refused a more prestigious one at a boarding school for family reasons. However, she is unmistakeably a 'lady' (her father, deceased, was a Nonconformist minister), and it is poverty alone which causes her snobbish schoolfellows to look down on her. Similarly, in *The Abbey Girls* (1920), Joan and Joy Shirley are impoverished 'ladies' and can only continue at school with assistance; readers will hardly need reminding that Joan refuses the offered Hamlet Club scholarship because Joy needs it more and that in the end Joy proves to be the heiress granddaughter of a wealthy baronet.

Angela Brazil, rather similarly, has a scholarship girl as the heroine of *The Luckiest Girl in the School* (1916); again, Winona is emphatically a 'lady', but family reverses mean she can only go to school with a scholarship. Brazil does not even allow her scholastic brilliance: Winona is awarded her scholarship originally through a mistake, and is only allowed to keep it because her historical essay shows imagination.

The winning of a scholarship to keep a girl at school is an important factor in *The New House Captain* (1928), the first of Bruce's Springdale series, where Diana Stewart's withdrawal from all extra commitments in order to concentrate on her scholarship work causes most of the new captain's difficulties as well as personal heartache.

I shall mention only three other examples by moderately important writers: Irene Mossop's *Well Played, Juliana!* (1928) has scholarship Jesmond at a very small and rather exclusive private school. Her schoolfellows' attitudes are rather more realistic than Elder depicts those of Monica's to be, though she suffers exactly the same shabby-dressing-gown problem as Monica does and has more consistent difficulties caused by having less money than the other girls. Mossop, however, goes for the melodramatic solution: Jesmond (who is, incidentally, not working class but impoverished middle-middle class) turns out to be the twin sister of the wealthy new girl Juliana. In rather the same way, Winifred Norling's Tansy (*The Testing of Tansy*, 1939), after battling through her scholarship difficulties, turns out to be an adopted child and is restored to her eminent and wealthy relations. Christine Chaundler's *Sally Sticks It Out* (1924), which is a year earlier than *The Scholarship Girl*, has a heroine who endures all sorts of vicissitudes before the final revelation sets all right; it is notable that this book may have been the model for Denise Deegan's wonderfully funny (and astutely observant of the genre) play, *Daisy Pulls It Off*.

Elder's book could not have been turned into a farce, and nor could any by the writer who above all used the theme of the scholarship girl in the most realistic manner. It is with Winifred Darch that we get the real scholarship girl, for she has a fine range of them, undoubtedly drawn from her own experiences as pupil at Leytonstone High School and staff member at Loughton High School, and she presents them well and without exaggeration. The scholarship girl of lower social status had become a real feature of high schools following the 1921 Education Act, which did not introduce the idea of scholarships but for the first time made real provision for them. Darch must have seen the results at first hand, and within three years had written *Heather at the High School* (1924), which has a younger child as protagonist. So too does the much later *The Scholarship and Margery* (1938), while *The Lower Fourth and Joan* (1930) ingeniously translates an ancient benefaction designed for apprenticeships into a scholarship. Perhaps more typical of Darch's best work is *Gillian of the Guides* (1925), which features working-class Ivy, reluctantly Head Prefect and Guide patrol leader, tactfully befriended by Gillian, daughter of a gentleman farmer and of impeccable lineage. Ivy's relationship with her own family is nicely portrayed, as is her real difficulty in dealing with girls of her own age and class who are already working. Later, *Margaret Plays the Game* (1931) has as a minor character lower-middle-class Midge, who is brainy but scruffy and has to be reformed in much the same way as do some of her working-class scholarship sisters. Probably the best of all in its depiction of the social implications of scholarships and high schools is *The New School and Hilary* (1926), where we have one adult speaking her mind about high schools:

> "What can people expect who send their daughters to such places! ... They associate with all sorts of people who have no idea of refinement. They get a lot of book-knowledge in their heads, no doubt, and are crammed up for all these exams., being taught by over-paid teachers at the expense of the poor ratepayer."

This is not dissimilar to the idea behind Elder's picture of Monica: book-learning at the cost of refinement, though Elder underplays Monica's lack of polish and stresses the importance of cultivating the whole person.

By the time Elinor M Brent-Dyer came to tackle the scholarship theme the educational picture in England had changed. In the 1950s a scholarship girl was no longer remarkable in a state or direct-grant school, and the theme had reverted to its original form, that of the girl who needs a scholarship to go to, or stay at, a fee-paying, non-state school.

Rosamond Lilley, in *A Problem for the Chalet School* (1956), is given a private scholarship to the Chalet School, having failed to get a state scholarship to her local high school because of illness. She is rather in Monica's mould: working class, but with nice manners and habits, her mother having been in 'good' service; the problem of her outfit is solved by the nature of her scholarship, which provides for everything—of course in the best of taste. By contrast, Joan Baker, her erstwhile schoolfellow, comes to the Chalet School when her grandfather wins the pools, and displays all the (supposed) working-class mores of cheap or inappropriate finery (including permed hair) and an interest in the opposite sex. In this book it is nouveau-riche Joan, not scholarship Rosamond, who has to learn to conform, and the noble Chalet girls are of course more impressed by humble worth than by flaunted wealth.

It is interesting to contrast Brent-Dyer's scholarship girl with her friend Phyllis Matthewman's Rusty. *The Queerness of Rusty* (1941) belongs emphatically to the interwar period, when it was still just possible for a girl to leave school at 13 and go into domestic service. (The official school-leaving age was 14, but Matthewman used the loophole which allowed some children to leave earlier if their work was needed.) Rusty is adopted by a kind benefactress and sent to boarding school, where her attitudes cause more consternation than her slight accent. She is not technically a scholarship girl, but her situation is very similar and she makes quite a good fist of explaining why she is different: at only just 14 she has already been out in the world and learned to think in a more adult way. Because she appears older than she really is she has attracted the boys' attention and has even received proposals. Of course she has not accepted them, but even so her attitude to her male friends is different from—and more realistic than—that of the gently reared maidens among whom she finds herself. Joan Baker she isn't, but neither is she Rosamond Lilley.

It is hardly worth mentioning Enid Blyton's scholarship girl Eileen in her St Clare's series, or that Anne Digby conveniently impoverishes a father in her Trebizon one, since neither contributes anything fresh to the scholarship theme.

The last word, as one might expect on any school-story theme, is to be found in Antonia Forest, who tackled the theme of the girl who must win a scholarship to stay on at her expensive boarding school in *The Cricket Term* (1974), where the emphasis is on Nicola's feelings about the possibility of having to leave Kingscote. She certainly is motivated to work harder, and does satisfactorily achieve the form prize which ought to guarantee her success, but in the end it is only to see the scholarship awarded to her academically undeserving but dramatically gifted twin. As usual Forest revised and invigorated a standard plot, and used it as the vehicle for a complex investigation of character and emotions. Nicola is not, as it turns out, a scholarship girl, but the book makes it perfectly clear that more is at stake than merely a set of school fees. Nicola's future will not be wrecked if she has to leave Kingscote, nor will she sink in social status; it is the loss of her friends that troubles her, apparently even more than the prospect of being separated from her twin. And it is perfectly clear that it is Kingscote which will be the loser if Nicola has to leave prematurely.

Thus the scholarship-girl theme turned full circle. In the middle stands the idea of social advancement through superior education, which the high-school-educated Elder knew all about. It is to her credit that she also saw that a 'better' education had to be not merely scholastic but also holistic, and this Monica, her scholarship girl, most effectively demonstrates.

Hilary Clare
2011

PUBLISHING HISTORY

The Scholarship Girl was published by Chambers in 1925 and appears not to have been reissued.

The illustrated front board is reproduced opposite. The dustwrapper illustration is reproduced on the front cover of this GGBP edition, and a copy of the spine appears on the back. Since the original book had no blurb, we have supplied one.

Hilary Clare and Sarah Woodall
2011

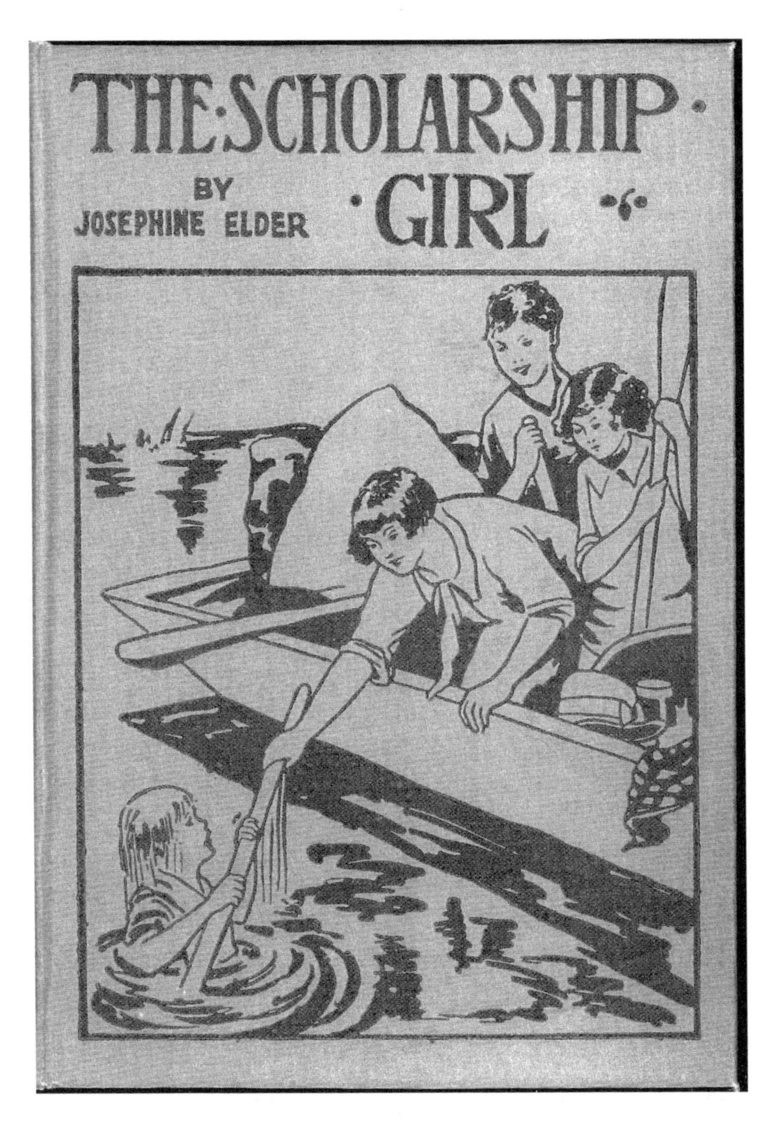

Front board of the first edition

NOTE ON THE TEXT

For this Girls Gone By edition of *The Scholarship Girl* we have used the text of the first edition, which contained several stylistic inconsistencies, a few typographical errors and some unusual spellings. This note explains what we have done about those we have found; we hope we have not introduced any new problems.

Where hyphenation and capitalisation were inconsistent we have standardised on the more usual version. We have therefore changed one 'back line' (in tennis) to the usual 'back-line', one 'dressing gown' to 'dressing-gown', one 'every-one' to 'every one', one 'games mistress' to 'games-mistress', one 'Mason's house' to 'Mason's House', three occurrences of 'bath-room' to 'bathroom' and eight occurrences of 'anyone' to 'any one'.

There was one instance each of 'forward-line' and 'forward line', which appeared close together on pages 75 and 76. Because of their close proximity, we decided to make an exception to our usual rule (of changing such things only when we can determine a clear majority usage) and standardise on 'forward-line'.

Elsewhere there were also one 'hockey field' and one 'hockey-field', one 'pillow fight' and one 'pillow-fight', and two occurrences each of 'kitchen garden' and 'kitchen-garden' and of 'tennis court' and 'tennis-court'. However, as all of these pairs are widely separated in the text we have left them alone.

There were two occurrences of 'farm-yard' and two of 'farmyard', plus one that was broken over the end of a line, so it was not possible to determine which was the real majority usage.

We have corrected punctuation only where it is clear that a mistake was made in the original, inserting missing closing quotes at the ends of speeches in five places.

The spellings 'straightway', and 'moral' are unusual but acceptable variants of 'straightaway' and 'morale'. The word 'scunner', which appears once (on p57), is a chiefly Scottish word that means 'a strong dislike'.

The words 'wabble' and 'wabbled' both appear, indicating that this probably was the author's choice of spelling. There is also one occurrence of the more conventional 'wobbled'.

In the original, 'Between-whiles' on page 65 appears as 'Between - whiles'.

Queens' College in Cambridge usually has the apostrophe at the end of its name (signifying that it was founded by two queens), but in this book it appears consistently as 'Queen's', and we have not interfered with that.

'"Ten little nigger boys"' on page 131 would not, of course, be acceptable if used by a modern writer, but it is in quoted text and it was commonplace when this book was originally published, so we have left it unaltered.

Sarah Mash and Sarah Woodall
2011

The Scholarship Girl

BY

JOSEPHINE ELDER

Illustrated by
ROSA C. PETHERICK

CONTENTS.

LIST OF ILLUSTRATIONS.

THE SCHOLARSHIP GIRL

PROLOGUE.

'AND we have to congratulate Monica Baxter on winning the open scholarship to Greystones School. Hip, hip—'

''Ooray! 'Oo-oo-ooray!! 'Ray!!!'

The children of St Barnabas Church School, Enford, led by the head-teacher, howled their approval.

'You have my best wishes for a good holiday. One—two—three!'

The school turned sharply to the right and scuffled out. They struggled in the little stuffy cloakroom for hats, coats, and satchels, and shouted raucously to each other.

''Bye, Edie!'

'Mary—wait—for—mee!'

'Well, chin-chin, ol' thing!'

'Good-bye-ee!'

Many of the older girls were leaving, some to go into offices, some home to help mother, some, rather ashamed of themselves, into service. They lingered, loth to say good-bye to the old life, yet eager, many of them, to grow up and become, as they imagined, independent.

A group was gathered round one of the windows; at its centre a slim, rosy-cheeked girl whose dimples came and went as her eyes travelled, twinkling, from one face to another.

'How did you do it, Monica?'

'D'you want ter go there? It's *awfully* grand, Monica! There's an 'onerable there, I know. Mother says so! She—she was a maid there, onct!'

'Oo, you'll still be at school when I'm earnin' three poun's a week dressmakin'!'

'You won't know us, Mon!'

The slim girl drew her brows down over her deep-set eyes and stamped her foot. 'I *shall* know you, Edie Simpson! I sha'n't get grand! I—oh, I don' know if I wanter go!'

''Course you want to! You always was fond o' books—an' you're grander'n us already! You *speak* different, some'ow, an' look different, in spite o' yer clo's!'

'Do I? I don't think I do. I say, I've got to have *such* a lot o' clothes, Edie! They sent mother a list!'

'Monica—Monnie—let's come an' see 'em before you go!'

'Yes—let us!'

They pressed round her, and she waved her black bobbed head. 'Rather! You shall *all* come! I'll come 'long an' tell you when. I say, I've got to go to Miss Elman before I go home. S' long—see you presently!'

She elbowed her way through the crowd, and stretched her long legs in their darned brown stockings to take three steps at once as she bounded upstairs. She knocked decorously on the head-teacher's door, and went in when she heard Miss Elman's voice.

The mistress was gray and thin, the weariness of her face making her look twice her age. She looked up at Monica without any great interest. 'There are just a few things I ought to say to you before I see the last of you,' she said.

'Yes, Miss Elman.'

'You'll find it very different from this.'

'Yes, Miss Elman.'

'That,' the mistress said sharply, 'is one of the first things you'll have to change. *Don't* say my name every time you speak to me!'

'No, Miss El—. It sounds so rude not to!' the girl explained.

'It's not done. You'll find a lot of things that you do are not done, I'm afraid. I'd no idea you'd pull the thing off, or I'd have taken you in hand before this. However you did it I don't know!'

'Father's taught me a lot at home, M—'

'Thank goodness you don't just say Miss, anyway! I've taught you that much.'

Monica shifted her feet and smiled.

'One thing I wanted to tell you was this,' Miss Elman went on. 'Don't be tempted to dissipate your energies. You'll find girls there who do nothing at all, learn nothing at all. Some waste their whole time on games. Don't do that. Stick to your work. You're not like them. When they leave they'll go to rich homes, or to college just for the fun of it. If you go to college, it'll be on scholarships. And to get scholarships you've got to work. You've got good brains, Monica. Don't waste them; don't be tempted to waste them. It's work for you, not play, till you've earned it. That's all. Good-bye, and good luck!'

She held out her hand, and Monica gripped it, solemn-eyed, and went to join the other girls in the grubby East London street.

CHAPTER I.

NEW CUSTOMS.

THE bell jangled up and down the corridors in Mason's House at Greystones School. Away in the other houses the tinkling passage of other bells could be faintly heard. The little world of the school was being shaken into action, mistresses and girls alike rubbing drowsy eyes and stretching sluggish limbs full of holiday languor, unwilling to enter on the strenuous days of term again.

Monica Baxter swung her long legs out of bed at the first clang. Where was it that she had seen that bathroom last night? Was it to the right or to the left along that tremendous long passage? One could have a bath every single morning if one liked, as long as one came down in time for breakfast.

She struggled into a dressing-gown, seized her sponge and towel, and peered this way and that from her door. No one was to be seen, nothing heard except low rustlings and grumblings as the occupants of the little rooms forced themselves to wake up.

She saw a door on the other side of the passage, a little way along. That must be the bathroom that she had seen. She darted to it, and shut herself in. There was no sign of human occupation except the water which trickled into the bath from the cold tap.

Monica turned both taps on full and jumped in. It was a lovely bath, warm and sparkling. She scrubbed and splashed and grunted, and jumped out in a hurry to rub herself all red and tingly. It *was* exciting, this great new school on the South Downs, with its big clean rooms and open windows through which the thyme-smelling wind blew. She wondered if the girls often went to the seashore, two miles away. She had arrived late last night and had not seen any of them. They would be quite different from the Enford girls, she was sure. She felt a little bit frightened of them. She was giving a final rub to her back when the door-handle was rattled peevishly, and a voice made a sound of surprise outside when the door remained closed.

'Who on earth—! Hi, what are you doing in there?'

'Drying meself!' Monica answered promptly.

'Who are you? Open the door!'

'Can't. I'm not decent yet!' Monica told her in shocked tones.

'Well, who are you, anyway?'

'Monica Baxter.'

'Never heard of you. Do be quick.'

Monica scuffled into some clothes, caught up her towel and pyjamas, and came out. Lolling against the wall was a tall, thin girl with a fair plait, the neatness of which struck Monica as extraordinary for that time in the morning. They stared at each other.

'You're new, I gather,' the fair girl said, 'or you'd know no one's supposed to bath before the dormitory prefect—that's me. And you bagged my bath.'

Monica considered. 'Well,' she said, 'I was here first.'

'That's what you ought not to be,' the other snapped. 'You ought to wait till I've been.'

Monica felt argumentative. Why, she could have had her bath and been fully dressed before this person had appeared, if she had only hurried a little. And she said so.

The other girl waved her sponge crossly. 'Doesn't matter if you could! D' you think I want to wash in a bath where your dirty feet have been?'

Monica's dimples came. 'I washed it out!' she objected stoutly.

'I don't care *what* you did! You're not to bath before the prefect!'

Monica started away along the passage. 'I shall!' she called over her shoulder—'if the prefect doesn't get up earlier!'

The other girl disappeared into the bathroom in a whirl, and Monica discussed the matter with herself as she finished dressing. 'I s'pose,' she said to herself, 'that's one of the things Miss Elman says "aren't done!" Well, I'm just jolly well goin' to do it, if I want to. Who does she think she is? Shouldn't get a bath at all if I waited till she'd done!' She surveyed herself in the glass before she went downstairs. She saw quite a new Monica, slim and sleek in her well-cut red tunic, her long legs in black stockings without a single darn, her feet in new, flat-heeled slippers. She gave an extra brush to her hair; it was straggly and did not quite fit in with the rest of the picture. She joined the throng of other sleek red figures running down the stairs.

At breakfast the room seemed full of people, all chattering, indistinguishable from each other except by the colour of their hair. Monica sat quietly, watching and listening, wondering whether she would ever know any of them by name. The girl next to her passed her food politely enough, but was too busy talking to her neighbour to devote much attention to the new girl. Monica did not mind. There was so much to see and to get used to.

After breakfast the juniors were turned loose in the big bare Junior room, to find lockers for themselves and pack their books into them, copy time-tables, and generally arrange their belongings. Each new girl, as she went in, was kept for a minute or two by a mistress, who told her what form she was to go to, and where her form-room was.

'Monica Baxter? Oh yes … Lower Fifth; science side. Your room's on the right-hand side of the big corridor on the ground floor. I'll find some one to show you. There's Marjorie Taylor.—Marjorie! Show Monica Baxter the way to the Lower Fifth when you go along, will you? There are only two new girls in the form, and she's one. Thank you.'

Marjorie gave Monica one glance. 'Meet me at the door here when the bell goes,' she said, and rushed away.

Monica found an untenanted locker and began to stow things in it. She saw an older girl, broad and brown-faced, with corn-coloured hair cut straight above her neck, come in and prowl round the room. Presently she seemed to catch sight of Monica, and made a bee-line for her.

'New girl?' she inquired.

'Yes. Monica Baxter.'

'How old?'

'Fourteen.'

'Fourth Remove?'

'No. Lower Fifth, they told me.'

The girl grunted. 'Bit young. S'pose you're brainy. Well, I'm Erica Pulteney—games captain. Just tell me what games you've played before, will you, please?'

Monica sat back on her heels and shook her black hair. 'I'm not goin' to play any games!' she said.

The captain stared at her. 'Why ever not? Doctor's certificate, or something?'

'No. I'm just—not going to.'

'Every one plays games!' the older girl told her patiently. 'It doesn't matter if you haven't played before. One soon learns.'

'I have played before. I don't want to.'

Erica stared at her. 'You'll find it awfully dull if you don't,' she warned her. 'There are only about five people in the whole place who don't, and they're always ill. You're not ill, are you?'

Monica smiled. 'No. Never!'

'Well, let me put you down to play hockey. Or lacrosse, if you'd rather. I expect you've played hockey before, though.'

'I'm not goin' to play games, thank you very much,' Monica said, politely and finally.

The other humped her shoulders. 'Well, if you won't, I can't make you. If you change your mind, come an' tell me.'

She went away, and Monica saw her talking to another younger girl, who turned and looked at Monica and laughed.

Monica felt rather regretful. She had enjoyed hockey at Enford. She would have liked to play, and liked to please this thin-faced, pleasant captain who made it her business to ferret out new girls and tell them what 'everybody' did. But Miss Elman's warning stuck in her head. 'Don't dissipate your energies … It's work for you, not play, till you've earned it.' Suppose she never earned it till she was too old to want to play. That would be dreadful. But she must not forget, she told herself, that she was different from these girls. She was the first scholarship girl they had ever had. She was different from every single one of them. She was a worker … They were all going to be just ornaments, people who did as they pleased and never wanted things. She must work.

Erica, the games captain, turned at the door and looked at the new girl's back. She would have a nasty time, with her queer, Cockney voice, and her defiant eyes and self-will. Erica knew she was the scholarship girl. The senior prefects had been told about her, and asked to keep an eye on her. The juniors, among whom she worked, were told nothing at all. With them she had to find her own level, unhindered and unhelped.

As the days went on, Monica decided definitely that she did not like these girls. They were so restrained and polite. They talked in little, mincing voices. They all used the same words, and all wore the same clothes, and did the same things at the same time, and did exactly as they were told. There were no bursts of noise, as there might have been any minute at St Barnabas. She felt instinctively that they attached great importance to one's outside. They couldn't make remarks about clothes, because every one wore the same. But she was sure they criticised people's voices rather than the things they said, and thought a polite turn of speech more important than a good turn to some one else. And they were enthusiastic about such silly things! Games, for instance, seemed to occupy all their thoughts. She had seen some of them leaving the pavilion for the hockey-field, and all their faces were serious and set, and they walked with tremendous dignity instead of skipping and pushing each other. Even when they were playing, the whole game was sometimes stopped so that the mistress who coached them might instruct them on some mysterious subject called style. When somebody played well, the mistress called out 'Pretty, pretty!' instead of 'Well played!' or 'Cleverly done!' That, she thought, was typical of them. The only things they worried about were appearances and play. They hadn't learnt yet that work and getting on in the world were the only things that really mattered. Of course, she reminded herself, they wouldn't have to get on in the world. They were 'on' already. They were not like her. And she would never, never, never let herself be like them.

She watched them out of her deep, defiant eyes and kept herself aloof from them. They tried to talk to her, but all their talk was of games, and she was not interested, and made no pretence of being. The few other girls who did not play were fully alive to their loss, and listened respectfully, and even hazarded remarks of their own when the play of this or that prospective member of a team was discussed. Monica curled her lip and looked out of the window or walked away.

The thing that irritated her most of all was the sight of members of the teams padding round the playing-field before breakfast or in the late afternoon on days when there were no games—'to keep fit.' She asked herself again and again what was the point of doing these nasty, uncomfortable things. It was just because somebody else did them, she decided. Some one had begun to do them years and years ago, and no one was bold enough to stop. It was the custom, as were so many other things at Greystones, and that was enough. Monica snorted. She almost wished she hadn't won that scholarship, except when she was at work, puzzling over algebra equations or boiling things up in the wonderfully equipped school laboratory. The scientist father of a late pupil had given the labs to the school, and they were unique in their way. Monica had already made up her mind to make full use of them.

CHAPTER II.

CONFLICT.

MONICA felt that she had scored over the question of morning baths. Every morning since the first she had waked up before the bell went, and had been in and out of the bathroom and back in her own room before the prefect had appeared. She had mopped out the bath very carefully, and she didn't think the prefect knew she had been there at all. She grinned with pleasure when she thought about it. There was no need to come to blows with these people, although she was quite prepared to do so if occasion demanded it. One just had to use one's brain. They, poor things, had let their brains go to rack and ruin.

On the eighth morning or so she did not wake quite so early as usual. Indeed, the clang of the bell broke rudely into a dream. She sprang out of bed and rushed along the passage.

Somehow, that day she could not hurry. All her fingers were thumbs. Perhaps they were sleepy. In any case, the prefect rattled the handle of the door before Monica was out of her bath. She felt a pleasant thrill of excitement. She had hardly spoken to any one during the past week. Now, at least, she would have a chance to tell somebody what she thought of her. She dried herself leisurely and pulled on her clothes, and then marched out.

The prefect was angry. She had been kept waiting quite a considerable time, and by a new girl. 'I thought I explained to you,' she said, turning a cold face on Monica, 'that you are not allowed to bath before the prefect.'

'You did,' said Monica jauntily. She was not going to be sat upon.

'I thought you understood.'

'I did.'

'Will you, please, not do it, then?'

'I shall do it,' Monica told her, 'just as often as I like. I've done it every single day.'

'I knew that,' the prefect said disdainfully. 'The windows were all shut, and you left splashes about. I *believe* you have a *hot* bath.'

Monica was indignant. She had been so careful to leave the room tidy; she certainly had forgotten about the windows. Her pride was hurt. 'Didn't!' she said viciously. 'Sausage-face!' She wrinkled up her nose and put out her tongue.

The prefect raised an astonished eyebrow and retreated with dignity, and Monica danced along to her room.

Later in the day she found a note sitting on her desk. It was a summons to attend a meeting of senior prefects in the head prefect's room at five o'clock in the afternoon. At first she was terrified. What was going to happen to her? She wouldn't go. She would go away somewhere by herself where they could not find her. Then she thought it over. If she didn't go, they would say she funked. She didn't funk; she only thought they were silly. Besides, they would catch her some other day if they didn't to-day. So at five o'clock she knocked at the head prefect's door and walked in. The six senior prefects of Mason's House were gathered there, standing and sitting in a group round Evelyn Standish, the dark, eager-faced senior who ruled the house. Her enemy of the bathroom was there, and Erica, the games captain, and a fat, solemn-faced girl called Penelope, whom she had often seen with Erica and Evelyn. The others she did not know. She faced them sulkily. They were only girls; they couldn't expel her, as the mistresses could. They couldn't do anything to her. She didn't care about them, not the flick of a cat's tail.

Evelyn came quickly to the point. 'You're Monica Baxter—Lower Fifth?'

Monica nodded. 'Yes.'

'We've had complaints that you have defied a dormitory prefect. She told you of a certain rule about times for baths, and you have ignored the rule. That true?'

'Yes. At least, if you mean that she told me I wasn't to bath before she did. I've had my bath and been out of her way every day except to-day.'

'That,' Evelyn told her, 'isn't the point. She told you a thing, and you didn't do it. You're new, and you don't understand, perhaps. But we expect obedience to prefects.'

Monica stuck out her lower jaw. 'They should tell me to do sensible things, then,' she said. 'There's no sense in that bath rule. If she came along d'reckly the bell rang, she'd get her bath first. She doesn't, so I do. If I waited for her, some one else 'ud come, and then p'r'aps some one else still, an' I shouldn't get a bath at all.'

Evelyn's eye glittered. She hated opposition now just as much as she used to when she was fourteen herself. 'Nevertheless,' she said, 'while you remain in the school you will obey the school prefects. We aren't prefects for fun. We're prefects to teach you how to behave.'

'What'll happen if I don't?' Monica asked curiously.

'If you were in a boys' school, you'd get spanked. You're not, so unfortunately we can't spank you. But you'll find things will be unpleasant if you don't behave.'

Monica ruminated over that. Hints were more unpleasant than spankings, on the whole. But she didn't believe they could *really* do anything.

Erica was leaning down, saying something quietly to Evelyn.

Then Evelyn spoke again. 'You're new, and you've come from different conditions from most of us; that's why you don't see eye to eye with us. So we'll explain a bit and give you a chance. We're made prefects for various reasons: partly to keep you in order, partly to teach us how to rule. But we're, none of us, made prefects until we've shown that we're fairly sensible and can be loyal to the school. We know it's difficult, sometimes. It's only that we're asking you to do now. Do as the prefects tell you, just because they're officers of the school and know what's best for it.'

Monica thought for a minute. 'It's not best for *me* not to have a bath in the morning!' she said.

'You must take your chance for that. It's bad for you to grab for a thing just because you happen to want it.'

'And good for her to!' Monica nodded at the Dormitory E prefect disparagingly. 'H'm!'

'The best possible thing for *you* is to learn to do as you're told!' Evelyn snapped. 'And please remember that it's not done to call the prefects names. I think it would be better not to call *any one* by that particular name!'

Monica looked round. They were all very sleek and serious and important; the Dormitory E prefect was positively smug. She hated them. 'I called her sausage-face!' she spurted. 'And she *is* a sausage-face. Look at her! You're *all* sausage-faces! Except Erica,' she added magnificently, remembering the games captain's kind eyes on her first day at Greystones.

Erica's face underwent a sort of inward convulsion, and Evelyn's, as Monica's look returned to it, seemed to be regaining its normal shape with some difficulty.

'You're just being rude and vulgar now,' Evelyn told her

severely. 'Go away and be ashamed of yourself. And try to remember to behave like a Greystones girl, not a little gutter-snipe. That's all.'

Monica glared, but could think of nothing to say to their coldly averted faces. She hurried out, and banged the door to show them that she was not at all sorry.

The minute she had disappeared the prefects looked at each other in comical dismay, and then burst into shouts of laughter. They had been defied in their own stronghold. What would happen if she didn't obey them, she had asked. They were helpless. A visit to a prefects' meeting, a moral lecture from Evelyn, reduced most juniors to pulp, so well established and revered was their authority. To Monica, authority was nothing unless it could do her harm.

'We'll have to give her another lecture sometime,' Evelyn said, when they were serious again.

'And be very down on her for things we *can* punish,' some one suggested, 'just to show her we've really got some power.'

'Can't we get at her through the other juniors?' Penelope asked.

But Evelyn shook her head. 'She doesn't seem to mix with them,' she said.

'P'r'aps she's terrified of them,' Erica said, remembering her own first term with its accusation of being 'stuck-up,' when really she had simply not dared to open her mouth.

'I don't think so,' Evelyn decided. 'She's not that sort. She's just up against us all because we're different from the people she's used to. She'll have to be squashed, I'm afraid.'

'Pity she won't play games,' Erica said regretfully. 'She looks as if she'd be good, and they'd help her to settle down.'

'M'm.' Evelyn turned to the Dormitory E prefect. 'You'll have to get up earlier, you know, Mavis,' she said. 'The kid's not going to stop her little game, and you can't sit down under cheek like that.'

Mavis blew out her cheeks in injured dignity. 'That's just what she *wants* me to do!' she complained.

'Can't help that. It's your right to bath first, and it's your business to uphold that right. If you want to annoy her as a punishment, you can stay in the bath till ten past seven or so. That'll teach her.'

Mavis looked sulky.

'It's up to you!' Evelyn pushed her point.

'All right,' Mavis agreed. 'Only I probably sha'n't wake up.'

'I'll wake you!' Erica grinned. She had kept to the habit, when she came, fresh from Dartmoor, to Greystones, of rushing out into the open air before breakfast, ere any one else was up. 'Half-past six?'

'Oh, I say!' Mavis protested.

'All right, quarter to seven, then. Joke if you don't race her, after all. We can't make her stay in bed!'

Mavis grunted, and Erica chuckled wickedly.

'That's all, isn't it?' Evelyn's businesslike voice tried to bring the meeting to a close. 'Keep an eye on the wretched infant, every one, and don't stand any sauce.'

The three friends were left to themselves.

'She's not a bad kid,' Erica said.

'And Mavis's face really *is* rather like a sausage,' Evelyn added, twinkling. 'It's so long and fat and expressionless!'

Penelope gave a plump gurgle. 'She's a lazy thing,' she said, 'an' I don't wonder the infant doesn't think much of her. She's a rotten prefect, *I* think.'

The others nodded thoughtfully. This scholarship girl was going to be a trial to the already harassed rulers of Mason's.

CHAPTER III.

REVENGE.

MONICA, released, rushed out into the garden in a state of mingled rage and fear. She hated them all. She hated Evelyn, who had dared to call her a gutter-snipe, who failed to realise that a gutter-snipe was as far below her as she was below them, and farther. But most of all she hated Mavis, the Dormitory E prefect, Sausage-face, who had started it all. She *wouldn't* do as they all did, she wouldn't be like them. She would work and work and work, and make herself famous, and—patronise them. She smuggled an elementary physics book with her into the Junior room when every one was supposed to be amusing herself with some hobby or other, and sat hunched up with it in a corner. She spoke not a word to any one before she went to bed.

In the morning she sprang up and rushed to the bathroom. The door was shut, and a sound of splashing and gurgling came from inside. 'Huh!' she comforted herself, 'I've made her get up early, anyway!' But when she had propped up the wall of the passage for twenty minutes, been passed by a dignified and perfectly expressionless Mavis on her way out, and had to hurry through her bath to a clamour from half-a-dozen juniors outside, she felt by no means so pleased. Mavis had scored. Back in her little room, Monica pulled on the rest of her clothes hastily, and ran down to breakfast.

A prefect at the bottom of the stairs stopped her. 'No house-tie! Go up and put it on, please.'

Monica looked down at herself. Stupid of her! She wondered

where it was. She hadn't seen it lying about. 'Won't it do after breakfast?' she inquired.

'No. Go and put it on now.'

Several other juniors looked curiously at her as they passed. She found herself racing upstairs again, almost against her will. She was quite tidy without the tie, she knew. What a fuss they did make about nothing. She found the tie, knotted it quickly, and just managed not to be late. After breakfast Mavis came up to her. 'Your room's in an awful mess,' she said severely. 'You'd better go up and tidy it before Matron sees it.'

She nearly said, 'Tidy it yourself!' But somehow it wasn't easy to be rude in cold blood with a crowd of girls behaving quite decorously all round her. She had the presence of mind to murmur, 'All right, Sausage-face,' as she went, and to notice that Mavis flushed angrily, although she appeared otherwise not to hear the remark. But she went obediently enough.

That was the beginning of a series of dreadful days. Whatever she did, wherever she was, a house-prefect bobbed up and criticised her, and told her to do some small thing or other. And, somehow, the habit of obedience was too strong for her, and she always meekly went off and did as she was told.

She began to realise how strong the prefects were. They all backed each other up, the traditions of the school helped them, and the other juniors unconsciously supported them. Mistresses were rebelled against, inefficient mistresses taken gleeful advantage of, but prefects were obeyed and respected.

Monica could not understand it. What was the good of obeying people who could not really punish you, whatever you did? But she obeyed them; and she hated them more than ever. They seemed like malignant fates who enjoyed taking advantage of her and leaving every one else's faults alone.

Events came to a point on a certain Tuesday, nearly three

weeks after the prefects' meeting. At the very beginning a prefect sent her upstairs to tidy her hair. She had been particularly careful with her dressing that morning, and she knew there was nothing really wrong with her appearance. Her hair just would not lie down; it never would. She tried to argue, but the prefect simply turned up her nose and repeated her command, and Monica wearily went. It wasn't any good trying to rebel, really.

Breakfast was a series of mishaps. She dropped her spoon into the big crock of porridge when she was helping herself to it, and was too shy to ask for another, so she went porridgeless. The next course was boiled eggs. And the evil genius which was in close attendance prodded her elbow as she was carrying her egg away from the hot-plate, and the egg danced on to the floor. It was a very soft egg. She was given another one, but she was made to feel very thoroughly in disgrace as well.

Lessons went badly, too. Somehow she could not concentrate on the problems about trains which passed each other and arrived at destinations at unknown times, and they came out quite wrong. At Latin she found, to her horror, that she had laboriously prepared the wrong chapter of Cæsar. And in her beloved lab a solution that she had made with great care and accuracy boiled over at her and ran away into the sink.

They had boiled mutton for lunch. She hated boiled mutton, and her spirits sank lower and lower. She listened to all the others chattering and asking unconcernedly for second helpings. The previous weekend had been the half-term, and most of them had gone home. She had not, because her parents could not afford the fare. They all had plenty to talk about. She would have liked to listen, but the juniors had quickly realised that this girl with the defiant eyes and the queer voice was no favourite of the prefects, and she was invited to join no group and included in no conversations.

She felt a sudden panic. She had meant so firmly to concentrate on work; but she had been thoroughly bad at it this morning. Suppose—suppose she never became famous after all!

She climbed up to her little room. Girls who did not play games had to lie down for half-an-hour after lunch with a book. Her book was a dull one, and she lay and brooded. How she hated Greystones and every one in it! Specially Mavis. It was queer how one hated people just because of their looks. Mavis had thick ankles, too. She could never like a person with thick ankles. She wondered what school would have been like if Mavis had not been there; quite different, she felt. She, Monica, would have come, and conquered at once. Every one would have liked her the minute they saw her. She would have been pressed into all the societies, and, since she would not play, have been urged to referee at games every day just because they liked to have her there. She would have refused, though. She would have gone away to a quiet place with a book—a work book—and learnt things, and become so palely studious that every one would have realised how learned she was and come to her for advice. And she would walk about—yes, she would—arm-in-arm with Erica and Evelyn and Penelope. Then the half-hour was up. She caught sight of her round face and sullen eyes in the glass. Pah! She hated herself too. She would never be learned at all. She couldn't, with that face.

She went downstairs towards the garden. The way out led through a conservatory, in which some of the experimental growing plants from the botany laboratory were kept. Peering through the glass doors, Monica saw a girl standing by one of the bell-jars under which the specimens lived; a girl with thick ankles and a smooth pink face, and a straw-coloured pig-tail with never a hair out of place.

With a plan hardly formed in her head Monica stopped at

the door leading from the conservatory to the house. Her enemy was there, by herself. What should she do to her? Something she must do, or she felt she would burst. Should she rush in and punch Mavis's nose? She might manage it—but Mavis was much bigger than she was, and it would be too humiliating if she ended on the floor with Mavis standing over her. Then she remembered how little the conservatory was used in the afternoon. All the school except a meagre half-dozen or so were playing games and would come indoors from the other side of the house.

Suppose Mavis had to stay there all night. She would simply hate that. And she Monica, would get her bath without any fuss in the morning.

She closed the door gently behind her, quietly turned the key and slid it into her pocket, and walked towards Mavis and past her. Mavis glanced up as she approached, but as soon as she recognised Monica, ostentatiously turned her back and became absorbed again in the plant before her.

Monica walked out through the far door. The gods were kind to her; the key was on the outside. She turned it, wrenched it from the lock, and tore down the steps in sudden fright. A few yards away she dared to look round. Through the glass walls she could see Mavis, still in the same position. She wriggled herself in between a tree and the garden wall and settled down to watch.

Mavis was tremendously interested in that plant; it seemed ever so long before she moved. Monica got quite tired in her cramped position behind the tree. Then, suddenly, Mavis plumped the bell-jar over the specimen and turned towards the house. She turned the handle this way and that, looked puzzled at the door, and then examined her own hands to see if they had grown suddenly weak. Monica, behind her tree, giggled nervously. Mavis rattled the door fiercely once or twice, then gave up the struggle and walked to the other door. She tried that in the same way, then scratched her eyebrow in perplexity. She walked along both sides of the long, narrow room; but none of the glass panes were made to open. She studied one of them for so long that Monica wondered whether she was meditating breaking it and jumping out. Monica hoped not; she might cut herself, and that would be Monica's fault. The hope was realised. Mavis shrugged her shoulders and sat down on the lowest of the shelves that ran along the side of the conservatory. She had evidently decided to await events, with her eye fixed on the house-door in case any potential rescuer should pass by. Monica watched her for a long, long time. Then she grew tired of it and whisked away, the keys jangling in her pocket.

She turned it … and tore down the steps.

CHAPTER IV.

A RESCUE.

MONICA wandered into the piece of waste land behind the kitchen garden. There was a haystack there, and a shed where the gardener kept his tools. The shed was built alongside a wall, and between it and the wall was a space about three feet wide. Standing at the opening of this space and peering along it was a girl. She was dressed in school uniform, but Monica did not remember ever having seen her before. She had thought she knew all the girls by sight now, even those who were in other houses. This girl was small and thin, and, seen from behind, looked about Monica's own age.

The girl turned as she heard Monica's footsteps, and looked at her with frank, eager eyes. Monica had certainly never seen her before. She had a little pale face with a bush of red-gold hair round it, a wide mouth over a little pointed chin, and great gray eyes which were the only things one noticed at the first glance. She did not look like a Greystones girl, in spite of the scarlet tunic and long black legs. She did not look at one superiorly and suspiciously, as all the others did. When she spoke there was a tinge of respect in her tone which made Monica's head go up on the instant. She had not been spoken to like that since she had questioned new girls at the Church School at Enford. The explanation came to her with a rush. New girls sometimes came to these big schools at the half-term; this must be a new girl. There was somebody newer and shyer than she was herself. She could have skipped for joy.

'I say!' The other girl was calling. 'Would you—could you help me?'

Monica came forward gravely. She had had so many rebuffs, she hoped this gray-eyed person also was not going to snub her.

'What is it?' she asked cautiously.

The other pointed towards the dark recess. 'There's a dog in there,' she said. 'He won't come when I call. He's been whining. I think he's ill.'

Monica peeped over her shoulder. Away at the end of the narrow space, against the wall that blocked it up, two eyes shone green. The dog, evidently a big one, was crouched as far from them as it could get. It stared at them silently. 'Perhaps,' Monica suggested, 'it's got rabies.'

'It might have,' the other girl agreed. 'They do go and crouch away by themselves then. Father taught me all the symptoms once, and that's one of them.'

'They're dangerous, aren't they, dogs with rabies?' Monica said.

'Yes. All the more reason to get it out.'

'Get it out?' Monica queried.

'Yes. I can't do it alone. It won't come, and I'm not strong enough to pull it.'

'Have you tried?' Monica asked in amazement.

'Yes. It didn't snap or anything. It just wouldn't come. Its nose is hot.'

'Did you go down there after it?' Monica persisted.

The other girl shook her head impatiently. 'Of course I did. Will you help me with it, please?'

'Don't you think,' Monica said, 'that we ought to put on thick gloves? And long coats, or something? I mean, if it's really got rabies, there's no sense in getting bitten.'

The other girl considered. 'No. I s'pose there isn't. It isn't brave to get wounded when you needn't; it's silly, my father says. Let's go and get them.'

'S'pose it gets out while we're away?'

'I don't think it will. Gardener's boy says it's been there three days, without any food.'

'Why didn't he get it out?' Monica inquired.

The other girl shrugged her thin shoulders. 'Frightened, I suppose. Come on—I mean—won't you come and get the gloves?'

They set off together towards the school buildings. 'You're new, aren't you?' Monica ventured.

'Yes, very. I only came the day before yesterday. I ought to have come at the beginning of the term, only I got measles.'

'Bad luck,' commented Monica.

'That's why I'm not playing hockey,' she went on. 'I'm not allowed to play games until next term.'

'I don't play at all.' Monica felt queerly anxious as she made the confession. She did not want this new girl to despise her, as the others seemed to. But the girl only raised sympathetic eyes to Monica's face, and repeated Monica's own remark, 'Bad luck!'

And Monica, for some reason, did not tell her defiantly that she had given up games from choice, not from necessity. She sought in her mind for some other subject for conversation, and remembered that her companion was newer than she was. 'What's your name?' she asked.

'Francesca Lucas. Will you tell me yours, please?'

'Monica Baxter.' The reverent turn of her companion's question warmed Monica's heart again, and her curly smile and her dimples came as she looked down on the mop of hair at her shoulder. 'Yours is a very funny name. Are you called all that?'

The other nodded. 'Yes, most times. It's after St Francis of Assisi. I'd like'—she glanced up and the gray eyes met Monica's brown ones—'to tell you about him, one day. Unless you know about him already,' she added with anxious politeness.

Monica shook her head. 'Never heard of him. But I'd like to hear about him—one day.'

At the door of Mason's—not the conservatory door by which Monica had come out—they separated. Monica flew upstairs and pulled out a pair of thick brown leather gloves with gauntlets, and a long mackintosh. She hated that mackintosh. Her mother had said that it would cover her in nicely, and she would grow to it, but it looked like a dun-coloured nightdress. However, its length would be useful now. She sped downstairs again and out across the garden by the way she had come.

Francesca was there before her, furry-backed gloves making great paws at the ends of her thin arms, cricket pads on her legs. 'Wasn't that a good idea?' She danced clumsily to show off her legs. 'Only, I mustn't turn my back on the enemy, or he'll have my calves.'

'I think,' Monica said briskly, hiding the terror induced by those green shining eyes at the end of the dark passage, 'I'd better go in and haul him out, if you can't manage him. I'm a good bit bigger than you. Then you can hold him while I scrabble out myself.'

Francesca nodded agreement. 'If you don't mind. I don't think there's room for both of us.'

So Monica dived along the twenty yards or so of dank, gloomy passage, from which the light was shut out by the overhanging roof of the shed. The dog just watched her. 'He's not growling,' she called encouragingly.

'He's only frightened,' Francesca called back.

She stretched out a hand and held it in front of the animal's nose. 'He's a sheep-dog; a bob-tail,' she said.

'I know,' said Francesca.

'Oh—he's licked me!'

The pointed nose had come hesitantly forward, and a hot, dry tongue had touched her gloved hand.

‘That’s all right. He’ll come with you now—if he can.’

‘He can’t,’ Monica said positively. The dog had tried to stagger to his feet, but had fallen back whimpering on his haunches. ‘I’ll have to drag him.’ She took the broad collar in her hands and tugged, and the dog, doing his valiant best, lurched forward. Several times he sank down and she could not raise him, but always after a little rest he was willing to come on. At last they reached the opening, and Francesca’s long hands joined Monica’s at the poor beast’s neck.

‘Let’s take him to gardener’s cottage!’ Francesca said; ‘he’ll know what to do.’

Monica looked doubtful. The cottage was some distance away, and the gardener was a sour-looking man. ‘Will he?’

‘Course he will. Gardeners always do.’

They turned the dog over on his back; he pawed the air feebly, but did not resist. Taking him up like an enormous baby, they set off crab-wise along the path.

Outside the little garden Francesca paused. ‘We’ll leave him here. Gardener’s got a dog, and this one’s p’r’aps infectious. Will you stay with him?’

Monica stayed, with a hand on the rough, furry neck. Francesca disappeared without hesitation into the cottage, and came out in a minute with the big man at her heels.

‘Got that great beast out, did ye?’ he said. ‘Well, you’ve got pluck.’ He looked down at them with twinkling eyes. ‘’E might ’ave bit you.’

‘He couldn’t,’ Francesca said triumphantly, dancing on one leg, her gray eyes glinting. ‘We put on gloves and—and things!’

‘So ye did. Ye’ve got sense, too,’ he allowed. ‘Well, let’s look at ’ee.’ He bent down over the dog, and it looked up at him, showing white half-moons in its eyes, but not attempting to snap. ‘’E’s only a pup,’ the man said. ‘Nigh full-grown, but still a pup. ’Appen ’e’s got distemper.’

‘Not rabies?’ they cried together.

He looked at them with a slow smile. ‘Don’ think so, missie. Did ye think ’e ’ad?’

‘Thought he might have!’

‘Ye’ve got—pluck!’ he muttered again. ‘No; ’e’s got distemper, I reckon. Got it bad, too. Fair starved ’isself. That’s what they allays do; feels ill an’ *won’t* eat, an’ then gets so weak they *carn’t* eat. ’E’ll want spoon feeding. ’E’s a good dog, though; worth saving.’

‘What’ll you do with him?’ Francesca asked.

Monica stood by, letting her do all the talking, and admiring her self-confidence.

‘Aw, I’ll put ’im in this barn. My dogs is all old dogs; they won’t take no notice o’ ’e. Keepin’ warm and feedin’; that’s what ’e do want.’

‘And when he’s better?’

‘Time enough, missie. ’E won’t be well for a long time yet. Time to find out who ’e belongs to.’

‘I hope,’ Francesca said, ‘that he doesn’t belong to anybody, then we can keep him for a mascot.’

‘Oh, let’s!’ Monica joined in.

They saw the sick animal comfortably tucked up in some hay, and watched the gardener go indoors to find hot milk for him. Then, with a pleasant sense of something accomplished, they turned away.

‘That was fun,’ said Francesca. Then—‘I like this place. Don’t you?’

Pride would not let Monica confess how very much she did not like it. ‘It’s a topping school,’ she temporised.

‘I’ve never been to school before,’ the other babbled on.

'My father's a professor at Cambridge, and he wanted to teach me himself. I learnt lots of things. But I expect you think I'm awfully green, don't you?'

Monica laughed. 'No,' she said; 'you don't seem green a bit.'

'Not really? I *am* glad. I thought I must be. I say, it was decent of you to help me. I wish I was in your form.'

'So do I,' Monica said fervently.

Francesca glanced up at her, beaming. 'How jolly nice of you! I don't expect you do, really. I don't expect you mind a bit. Doesn't matter. I suppose we've got to go in now.'

'I suppose we have,' Monica answered dully.

'I don't want to.'

'Nor do I!'

They smiled at each other shyly, and dived away in different directions.

'She doesn't know I'm new at all,' Monica told herself triumphantly. 'She doesn't know I'm—different.'

CHAPTER V.

AUTHORITY ACTS.

MONICA had changed her clothes and settled down to tea before she remembered Mavis. What an exciting afternoon it had been! She had disposed of an enemy, and perhaps made a friend. She took an enormous bite of bread and jam, and looked round benevolently on the company at the table. She did not care much what they thought about her just to-day; even if they did not think about her at all it didn't matter. She wondered what Mavis was doing. She stopped suddenly in the middle of the next bite. Poor Mavis, she wouldn't get any tea. She felt a little ashamed of herself, then thrust out her chin in defiance at her own softness. Why should Mavis have tea? She was a nasty, mean, superior thing, and Monica was glad if she had given her a dull afternoon. She hoped she would have to stay there all the evening, and all night as well. She would go round that way to get up to her class-room after tea, just to see how Mavis was amusing herself. She went; walking up the stairs and along the passage firmly, so that she would not look like a conspirator if any one met her. She need not have troubled. The conservatory door was wide open.

* * * * * *

Mavis had sat down, seething with anger, when she had discovered that she was a prisoner. She had realised at once that Monica was her jailer, and her rage was due even more to her dislike for the scholarship girl than to annoyance at the prospect of a wasted afternoon. A junior who dared to insult a prefect so was not to be tolerated. A scholarship girl with a Cockney accent and untidy hair, and no traditions but those of a National

School, who could be cheeky to, and even appear to despise, a young lady who lived in a mansion, and even owned a hunter and a little two-seater of her own, and had, moreover, a good enough brain to have attained to the sixth form at Greystones, was beyond her understanding altogether. She considered that the prefects had let her down when they had insisted that she should get up early. She wanted the privileges of a prefect; the responsibilities she preferred to do without.

She wondered what she had better do. It was very undignified to sit there until the chit of a junior should choose to let her out. But she could not possibly get out by any way except the door, so there seemed nothing else to do. She grew more and more angry as the minutes went by, each one longer than the one before. So that, when at last she heard steps on the stairs she banged such a furious tattoo on the door that the housemaid, going upstairs with a tea-tray, nearly dropped all the crockery on the floor. Mavis made her understand that she was locked in, and that the keys had disappeared. The maid, being a person of common-sense, went straightway to the housekeeper, that worthy appeared with a jangling bunch, and Mavis was very soon free. The housekeeper, a wise woman well used to schoolgirls, asked no questions, and vanished into her own domain.

Mavis hurried to the head prefect's room. This insolence must be put an end to, and Evelyn was the person to set in motion some scheme for Monica's suppression. She was a little put out to find Evelyn's two friends, Penelope and Erica, in the room with her. They had all just come in from games and were discussing teams. Mavis could manage Evelyn with a fair degree of ease if she was alone. She always had an uneasy feeling that Penelope's fat chuckle would break out against her the minute she had left the three of them behind; and Erica's stern common-sense she found devastating.

'Come in. You look peevish!' Evelyn said, as Mavis hesitated at the door. 'What's up?'

'It's—it's that little wretch, Monica Baxter!' Mavis exploded, her long face red with anger.

'Oh dear! I thought she was quelled. What's she done now?'

'She—she locked me in the conservatory passage and went off with the keys! I've been there all the afternoon!'

'What on earth did she do that for?'

'I don't know! Just revenge, I suppose. I was standing there looking at a plant, and she walked through. And when I tried to get out I found both doors locked!'

'So you're not even sure that she did it?' Erica said judicially.

'Nobody else went through!' Mavis asserted.

'But somebody else might have gone round—first to one door, and then to the other.'

'I'm perfectly certain nobody did. I'm *sure* it was Monica!'

'Well,' Evelyn said, 'supposing it was. What do you want us to do about it?'

'I think—she ought to be squashed.'

Evelyn ruminated. 'So she ought. I thought she had been.'

'Well, she evidently hasn't,' Mavis snapped.

'It seems to me,' Evelyn said, 'that she's got a private and particular scunner on *you*, Mavis. She's obeying the rest of the prefects jolly well, and not being a bit cheeky.'

Mavis glared at her. 'What d'you mean?'

'Simply that I don't see what we can do about it as prefects. There simply isn't anything we *can* do. It's no good just telling her she ought not to do it—she knows that quite well. Goodness knows why she did do it. If she was a boy, again, you could spank her. If she'd broken a rule we could give her lines. You can give her lines yourself, for cheek, if you like. If I saw her and gave her them she'd only think you were feeble not to do it yourself.'

'Isn't there anything else we could do?' Mavis wriggled uncomfortably.

'I don't think we can invent a punishment for that, do you? It really isn't serious enough.'

'Would you advise me to give her lines?' Mavis asked.

'Yes. I think I would, on the whole. She's not the sort of kid to ignore; she'd just think she had got off scot-free.'

Mavis went off, rather crestfallen and rather sulky.

'She's a bit of a trial, that kid,' Evelyn said, rubbing her chin.

'So's Mavis,' chuckled Penelope.

'I know. Still, one must stick up for a prefect.'

'The kid's better than she was,' Erica said. 'Much quieter and much less crude.'

'She's not a bad kid. At least, she's going to be,' Evelyn prophesied.

'I wish she'd play games,' said Erica. 'Then she wouldn't do these daft things.'

'I would like to have seen Mavis fuming in that greenhouse,' giggled Penelope.

Evelyn turned on her severely. 'Pen, you're bad; you're gloating.'

'I can't stand Mavis,' Pen confessed. 'But nobody knows except you,' she added. 'I'm as loyal—oh, as loyal as anything to every one else!'

The others laughed. Pen very seldom had her knife in people, but when she did, it stayed in and nobody could get it out.

* * * * * *

So it happened that when Monica met Mavis presently she found herself fixed with a stern, accusing eye. 'You'll write me fifty lines before to-morrow evening,' Mavis snapped. 'For cheek. Write "I must not be rude to prefects," and leave them in my room at tea-time to-morrow.' She whisked away before Monica had time to inquire what would happen to her if she did not do the lines.

CHAPTER VI.

ANOTHER RESCUE.

MONICA, having received her sentence, happened to walk through the gymnasium on her way to the Junior room. She had hardly shut the door behind her and advanced into the big room before she was greeted by a diffident 'Coo-ee!'

She looked all round the room. Some one must be hiding somewhere. It came again—'Coo-ee, Monica!' It was above her head. She looked upwards in amazement.

'Hullo! You, again!' she cried out involuntarily. For, astride one of the beams that ran right across the great room, her little face looking tinier and more elf-like than ever, sat Francesca.

'Yes,' came the answer, dolefully, 'me, again. I'm glad it's you.'

Monica grinned in spite of herself. 'What on earth are you doing up there?'

'I climbed up a rope.'

'We're not allowed on the apparatus except at classes,' Monica reproved. There seemed, she thought to herself, some sense in this rule which she had before thought funny and absurd. It was clever of the mistresses to have foreseen such a mad performance and guarded against it.

'I know. Some people in my form said I was too little to climb, an' I did it to show them I can climb like—like anything!'

'Why don't you climb down again, then?' Monica asked cruelly.

The pale face flushed, and Francesca shook her mop of hair. 'I—can't!' she confessed. 'I can't get on to the rope again. I—daren't leave go!'

Monica considered, her head on one side. 'P'r'aps if I came up too, I could help you,' she suggested.

'I wish you would. I'm a *little* bit afraid of falling off.'

So Monica heaved herself up hand over hand. She had attended gym classes in the Technical Institute at Enford, so she was quite at home. She hoisted herself on to the beam beside Francesca. It was very high. The mats on the floor looked the size of handkerchiefs, and the boards like narrow railway lines converging in the distance. She had better stop thinking about them.

'Can you get across the beam—on your front?' she asked Francesca.

'I—I think so.'

She wriggled and twisted her thin self, and presently the manœuvre was accomplished. 'Now,' Monica directed, 'get your legs round the rope. I've got you. Grip it, can't you, between your knees?'

The black legs waved, and in a minute circled themselves round the rope.

'Now, lower yourself by your arms. I've got you; you can't fall. You're awfully light. Now, take your right hand off the beam and grip the rope with it. Go on—I can't hold you all the evening!'

A second's hesitation, a frantic grab, and Francesca was sliding monkey-like downwards. Monica waited until she had reached the ground, and then followed, more slowly.

'That was jolly dangerous!' she said severely when she arrived at Francesca's side.

Francesca looked very meek. 'I know,' she said. Then, looking up at Monica with twinkling eyes, 'I s'pose you saved my life.'

'I—suppose I did. No, I didn't; you wouldn't *really* have fallen off.'

'I don't know about that. I was getting awfully giddy, and my legs were tired. *I* shall say you did.'

Monica grinned. 'You can *say* it,' she said. 'But I didn't, all the same.'

Francesca stamped her foot. 'I'm trying to say thank you,' she said, 'and you won't let me! Thank you—thank you—thank you! There!'

They glared at each other for a second and then threw back their heads in a shout of laughter.

'All the same,' said Monica when they had finished, 'I shouldn't do it again, if I were you.' She looked down at her companion, feeling more at home and more sure of herself than she had done since the days when she was 'top-girl' at Enford.

'Where are you going?' Francesca asked shyly.

'The Junior room.'

'Can I come with you? I'm always shy of going there by myself.'

'Yes, of course,' Monica said. Then she flushed a deep red. 'Only, I've got something to do when I get there,' she added.

'I'll help you,' offered Francesca.

'You can't,' Monica told her brusquely.

'Why not?' The persistent little person was skipping by Monica's side.

'It's—it's lines,' she said.

Francesca squeaked. 'How exciting! Have you been wicked? I love being wicked. I haven't had a chance since I've been here. What did you do?'

'I cheeked a prefect.'

'O-o-oh! I say! Why? What did you say to her?'

Monica's dimples came. 'Nothing. I locked her in the conservatory passage.'

'O-o-oh! You are brave! You're *always* being brave, aren't you?'

This was a new aspect of squashed Monica, and she laughed outright. 'No. It wasn't brave a bit. I was angry with her.'

'Why?'

So Monica told her the whole story, of the bath, and Sausage-face, and the prefects' meeting, and Mavis's hundred-and-one little snubs, and everything else.

'The horrid thing!' Francesca flashed; 'she does sound nasty! But—'

'What?' asked Monica as she paused.

'Nothing,' said Francesca.

They had reached the Junior room, and Francesca settled herself by Monica's side.

'Fifty isn't many,' she said.

And, somehow, it wasn't, with the little impish person making ridiculous comments as every line was done.

'What are you going to do now?' she asked, when the sheets were folded together.

'I generally read,' Monica said.

'Read what?'

'Work,' said Monica, colouring.

'Oh! How dull.'

'What do *you* do?'

'Draw,' Francesca answered promptly. 'Draw people. I'll go and get my things.'

She went across the room, and came back with an ordinary exercise-book of unlined paper. She handed it to Monica without the slightest self-consciousness, and Monica peeped at the first page.

'I—say!' she exclaimed.

The book was about half full. The first pages were covered

with sketches of country things—two cocks fighting; ducks waddling in a line; a pony; a sheep-dog and an Aberdeen; farm-boys haymaking and milking.

'That was a holiday,' Francesca explained.

Then came portraits; young men sprawling in chairs, and often an older man with a thin face and glasses.

'That's father, and some of the undergraduates,' she said.

There were young women, too, and a few children; and on the last used pages, girls in Greystones uniform, sitting about as they did in the Junior room, walking arm-in-arm, playing hockey.

'Why!' Monica exclaimed. 'There's Erica! And Evelyn! And—oh, heaps of people! And—and—isn't that me?'

It was Monica herself, curled up on a window seat. And she had not even known that Francesca existed.

The sketches were all in pencil, dark and firm, with the fewest lines imaginable; and every one could be recognised.

'They're simply wonderful!' Monica said.

'Oh, they're not. There are all sorts of things wrong with them, really.'

'Why don't you have a proper sketch-book?' Monica asked, surveying the tattered cover.

'I like this paper. It's smooth. Most sketch-books are rough, for painting, unless you get very expensive ones.'

'I see.'

Francesca began to draw, at first from memory. 'I get a sort of impression, like a photo, of a person just in a special position,' she said, 'like this.'

She drew what seemed to be, at first a medley of bent limbs, then put in a quick double stroke in the middle of it, and Monica recognised herself sliding down the rope in the gym.

'It's just wonderful!' she said again, and Francesca laughed with pleasure at the admiration in her eyes. It was reflected in her own. Where might she have been if Monica had not come up on to that beam?

She glanced round the room, and drew people here and there. Once or twice one would glance up and meet her eye, and stroll across to see what was going on. Francesca would look up frankly at her and laugh and go on drawing. Monica watched her, envying her lack of shyness. She had been at Greystones only three days to Monica's six weeks, and already she was on better terms with the girls than Monica was. She knew what to say and how to say it. Monica did not, and knew that she did not.

Between-whiles, Francesca and Monica talked. 'Why do you work when every one else is playing?' the former asked.

Monica grew pink again. 'I like working,' she said lamely.

Francesca said nothing, and Monica, suddenly ashamed of her reticence, amended, 'I want to work. I want to know everything. I want to—to be famous!'

'So do I,' agreed Francesca, scribbling. 'A famous portrait-painter.'

'I've *got* to be!' Monica insisted. 'I—I'm different from—from all the others!'

'Why?' Francesca inquired.

'I came here with a scholarship,' Monica announced, throwing out her chest like a little game-cock. It was not that she was proud of herself. Rather, she was afraid that her new friend would despise her, because she would know that a scholarship meant that Monica had come from a home very different from that of every one else.

But Francesca seemed unimpressed. 'So you've got to get another to go to college with,' she said. 'So've I. At least, I can't go without one. I would've tried for one to come here on if there'd been one. But there didn't seem to be from any of the Cambridge schools.'

'My school,' Monica said, determined to make a clean breast of everything now she had begun, 'was a National School.'

'Was it?' Francesca said politely. 'I thought National Schools didn't give one a very good education. You must,' she glanced up wonderingly, 'be very brainy to have got a schol. without a good education.'

Monica grinned. Francesca seemed determined not to despise her. Francesca looked up again, wondering if the silence meant that Monica was offended.

'I don't know anything about schools,' she went on. 'I've never been to one before. I told you so, didn't I? But father says that, about education.'

'*My* father,' Monica announced quietly, 'is a plumber.'

'He ought to be very rich,' Francesca said at once. 'People want plumbers all the year round. They only want professors during term.'

'He isn't,' Monica said, thinking of the little yellow villa wedged into a row, white steps climbing up to the door with variegated glass panels, windows from which aspidistras peeped between Nottingham lace curtains; and her mother, thin and always at work; and her father himself, going out on his bicycle with a bag of tools on his back, and coming in, dirty and cheerful, for his meals. 'He's not. We're awfully poor. That's why I have to get scholarships.' She was back at her first point.

Francesca came back to hers. 'You *must* be clever!' she said. 'We're poor, too. We're both poor, and we're both going to be famous. What fun!'

'I wish—' said Monica, and stopped, fearful at herself. The shadow of the strange place was still upon her. Then she remembered that Francesca was newer than she was. 'I wish we could do it together!' she said.

Francesca's blue eyes glanced up, unconcerned and sensible. 'Well, let's,' she agreed.

CHAPTER VII.

GOOD ADVICE.

MONICA at breakfast next morning saw Francesca, away at another table, laughing and chattering to the girls beside her. Would Francesca keep away from her now, she wondered, now that she knew all about her, and had had time to think it over? She could not have gone away last night without being rude, and Francesca was not the sort of person to be rude consciously. But to-day she could just avoid her new acquaintance, if she wanted to, without any trouble at all. Monica hoped quite wildly that she would not want to. But she wouldn't get in her way if she did. The two did not meet until break, for they were in different forms. Monica was wandering out to the garden when Francesca caught her up. 'Have you been to see how the dog is?' she asked.

Monica had not.

'Will you come?'

Monica would, and they set off for the gardener's cottage.

The dog was in the barn, tucked up warmly with some straw, asleep.

'Doan't wake 'e,' the gardener warned them. 'Sleep's the best thing for 'e now.'

'Is he better?' they asked.

'Yes. I got some egg an' milk down 'e last night, and some more this morning, wi' a drop of whisky to warm 'e. 'E's bin drinkin' watter by 'isself like a Christian, an' sleepin' like a babe. I think we'll save 'e, missie.'

They looked down at the patient silently for a minute or two, then left him alone.

'I do hope he gets better,' Francesca said. 'He looks very comfortable, though, doesn't he? It would have been miserable for him to be ill all by himself in that cold, dark place without any food.'

'I'm awfully glad you found him,' Monica said.

'And that you helped get him out,' Francesca added.

They walked back together, passing the tennis-courts on their way. 'I'm longing for the summer,' Francesca said, looking at them. 'I like hockey; but I do love tennis.'

'I love it, too,' Monica agreed, unthinking. 'I'm better at it than at hockey. There was a friend of my brother's who used to teach me.'

Francesca looked sympathetic. 'Did you hurt yourself, or were you ill?' she asked.

'Did I—what?'

'Is that why you don't play now?' Francesca explained.

Monica had forgotten. She coloured and hesitated, then spoke up. Later, she thanked her stars for the instinct that made her be honest to Francesca. Francesca could so easily have been deceived, for she was too honest herself to suspect dishonesty in others. 'No. I don't play games here because I want to give all my time to work.'

'But you can't work *all* the time!'

'I smuggle a book up to my room, or out here, when I get a chance.'

'But—don't you *like* playing games?'

'Rather—of *course* I do!'

Francesca shook her bushy head. 'I don't see what you mean!' she said.

Monica tried to explain. 'When I left my other school,' she said, 'the head-mistress told me I must work. Work hard and get on, and not waste any time over games or anything else.

She said people who played games a lot, like—like Erica, for instance—thought about games instead of work, and weren't ever good enough to get scholarships. You see, I'm different from the rest of you. She said so. I *must* get scholarships.'

Francesca flew into a rage. 'Why do you keep saying you're different?' she demanded. 'You're not. You're as ordinary—as ordinary as a turnip! Of course you've got to get scholarships! So've I! So've lots of the others! Only they don't make such a fuss about it, as if they were—sort of *anointed* to get scholarships!'

Monica stared at her. 'D' you think they have?' she said, wondering.

'Of course they have, if they want to go on to College. So you're not so different after all! Only when you make yourself.'

'Miss Elman *said* I was!' Monica persisted

'She probably didn't know anything about Greystones at all, or any other school either, except her own.'

'Don't *you* think I'm different?'

'You're a bit queer when you're with other people,' Francesca said, thinking. 'You never talk to them. You look—sort of proud. And you moon about by yourself in the afternoons. But then, so do I.'

'I never know what to say to people,' said poor Monica. 'An' if I do say things, I always think they're laughing at my voice.'

'Your *voice*?'

'It's—different from theirs.'

'Haven't you ever noticed,' Francesca asked, 'how an Irish person's voice is different from a Londoner's, or a Lancashire person's from a Cornishman's? It's only in children, or people who aren't educated, that the difference is marked. In ordinary grown-ups, you generally can't tell where they come from.'

'Well,' Monica grunted, 'I'm not educated. I know that.'

'That's what you're here for,' Francesca snapped; 'isn't it? It's what we're all here for.'

'To be rubbed down and made like everybody else! I *won't* be!'

'It's quite a good thing to be,' Francesca gave her opinion. 'It's much easier for people to get on together if they've all got more or less the same customs, and talk the same language. They can understand each other better, without taking so long to—to get through each other's shells. Don't you see? They needn't be the same inside, not a bit.'

Monica saw. 'I—s'pose not,' she allowed.

Francesca pushed her hands deep into her pockets and hunched her shoulders, a miniature edition of the professor, had she but known it. 'My father says,' she went on, 'that we don't come to school just to learn out of books. We come to learn to be people, too. To learn to control ourselves, and—get on with other people without rubbing them up the wrong way, and make ourselves as useful as we possibly can. *He* says we *ought* to play games, because you can't use your mind properly if you haven't got a healthy body, and games make it healthy. *Yours*'ll all go to jelly if you sit about an' work all the time. And then, games teach you not to lose your wool, an' not to cry when you get hurt, an' not to do things just for yourself—you know, like passing instead of keeping the ball.'

'I know all that,' Monica said sulkily, 'without any games. And I can't get on with people, anyway. Not these people.'

'You could, if you tried. You shut yourself up from them. You're not any *use* to them. If you're going to get on well in any place, you've got to be useful to it. Do things. Please people. You've got to give before you can take.'

That sounded sensible, Monica thought.

'I *shall* be useful to it, when I'm famous,' she objected.

'If you're going to wait till you're famous to have people talk to you,' said Francesca's detached tones, 'you'll find it awfully dull.'

'It *is* dull,' said Monica, 'horribly dull.'

'Well, you can stop it being.'

'How?'

'Get to know people. It's no *good* being famous if you can't get on with people. You can't teach them what you know if you don't like them, and make them like you.'

'I don't know how to get to know them,' said Monica miserably. 'I wish I did.'

'I should start by playing games and not being a crank. It's all bosh, what you say your school-mistress said. She didn't mean you to go dotty over work. She just meant you *not* to go dotty over games.'

'You're awfully wise,' Monica said.

'I'm not. It's father. He said all those things to me before I came.'

'*He's* awfully wise, then. No one said anything to me like that.'

'He is,' Francesca agreed fervently, 'the wisest person there is.'

'How do *you* know what to say to people?' Monica asked suddenly. 'You don't seem to mind what people are like. You just talk to them.'

Francesca looked pleased. 'That's like St Francis,' she said. 'He talked to everybody. He wasn't afraid of any one, and he didn't despise any one. I don't see how people *can* despise other people, do you?'

'I—don't know,' confessed Monica. She knew that she was afraid of a great many people, and took some pleasure in despising others to remind herself of her own importance. Francesca did not seem to think about her own importance at all. 'But one can't like *everybody*!' she said, harking back.

'*I* can—at least, unless they do something *very* beastly. I start off by liking them, I think.'

'I don't. I hated Mavis from the very beginning. There she is, the cow. Why *should* we have to obey people like that, and do lines for them? They can't do us any harm, even if we don't.'

Francesca laughed. 'Well, there's one jolly good reason for obeyin' them,' she chuckled.

'What's that?'

'You may be one yourself one day. And then, if you've helped people to—to not obey prefects just because they *are* prefects, you'll find they won't obey you either.'

Monica laughed too, tickled by the prospect. 'That's sensible,' she said. 'P'r'aps I'll obey 'em, then. Hadn't thought of it like that.'

'I've thought of something else,' Francesca said quickly. 'Look here, we both play tennis. Are you good?'

'Not bad,' Monica said, laughing still.

'Nor am I. Well, why shouldn't we be famous at that? You be famous at work and games, and I will at painting and games. There wouldn't be much we couldn't do, between us, then.'

'Could we?' Monica said doubtfully. 'People never *are* really good at two things, are they?'

'Sometimes. People at Cambridge are—get Firsts and Blues as well. Not often, but sometimes. Do let's try!'

'Come along in,' said Monica. 'It's time.'

CHAPTER VIII.

ST FRANCIS.

MONICA was more impressed by Francesca's wisdom than she had shown at the time. The more she thought about it, the more impressed she was. 'If you don't like people, they won't like you,' Francesca had said. 'And if you don't give, you can't take.' She was part of a great school, and in proportion as she helped it, so would it help her. She must think of the school, not of herself. She was only a little bit of it; a little bit which did not matter very much by itself after all. Her quick brain had seized on the fragments of philosophy which Francesca had learnt from her father and let fall in conversation, and had built them up into the very lesson that the professor had intended to teach.

'But of *course* one's got to do what's best for the school!' Francesca said, staring, when Monica faltered her discoveries to her one day. 'Every one does, doesn't she? There isn't any need to flap about it!'

Monica digested that, too. The point of view was natural to Francesca, natural to all the other girls who had grown up in it. To the scholarship girl, taught from the beginning that she must fight for herself and herself alone or she would be crushed, it was a new and absorbing idea. Her own career, her own future, had been so dinned into her mind that it had become, to her, the only important thing in her life. Now she saw, as through a suddenly-opened window, the larger future of the school and her own tiny efforts bound up with it. That was why the prefects were so decorous and magnificent; not because they thought themselves important, but because the outside world judged the school by them. And for the same reason they ground the rebellious, rackety juniors into submission. She had been looking at it all from quite a wrong angle. Now she saw it clearly.

But Mavis was not a proper prefect, all the same. She *did* think herself important. It was a pity; it somehow dimmed the glory with which, to Monica, prefects in general had become suddenly invested, to find one among them a human person.

'I s'pose I'd better stop thinking about her,' Monica told herself sensibly. 'She's a blot on the landscape. She's a— Oh, blow! she's a prefect.'

The outward sign of these inward convulsions was that Monica padded discreetly one evening to Erica's room, and found the games captain by herself.

'Please, I want to play games,' she announced, struck very shy and quiet. Erica was no longer an enemy, she was a deity who represented the school in the field.

Erica turned a friendly face to her. She had a fellow-feeling for silent, crotchety, bewildered new girls. 'That's good. What games, particularly?'

'Hockey, now, please. And tennis next term.'

'Keen on tennis?' Erica asked, scenting Monica's wish that next term would hurry up.

'Yes.'

'You'd better go in for the championships,' Erica advised kindly. 'There's always room for good juniors.'

'Francesca Lucas is keen on it, too.' Monica felt that she would be stealing a march on her friend if she left her name out.

'Is she? That's good. Well, hockey this term, you said. You'll find it a bit dull, if you're any use, because all the teams are made up now. Still, there's not very much of the term left, is there? You'd better turn out in the beginners' game this afternoon. I'm coaching it, so I shall be able to see what you're like. All right.' She turned to her book again, and Monica felt herself dismissed and faded away.

*　　*　　*　　*　　*　　*

Monica enjoyed the beginners' game very much at first. She was much better than any of the others, and, playing inside right, did some very showy runs down the field and shot several goals. She felt Erica's eye upon her and knew that she was shining among the crowd of slow, fumbling people, some of them older than herself. She loved shining.

Erica left her alone during the first part of the game. She coached some of the others vigorously; particularly a little, wiry half-back who was not on Monica's side. The result was that the little half attached herself very closely to Monica, and presently succeeded in getting the ball away from her.

Monica was annoyed. She had not thought very much of that half. She must pull up her socks. The next time the ball came her way she started off down the field with it. The half scampered after her and caught her up, and a tussle began.

'Pass!' adjured Monica's centre-forward frantically.

Monica did not want to pass. She was quite sure that, once free of the half who buzzed like a gnat round her, she could get the ball to the opposing goal much more quickly than the centre-forward could. She scrabbled and tapped with her stick, but every time she gained a little ground the half caught her up again and forced her to stop.

'Pass. *Pass!*' shouted the centre-forward.

The other half-backs of both sides began to hover close round. It would not be easy to pass now; nor to go on by herself, either. Her enemy, sticking like a limpet, gave a push and a twirl—and the ball sailed away to the opposing forward-line.

'D—!' swore Monica loudly.

The girls all round turned eyes of disgust and surprise upon her, then looked away.

Erica blew her whistle. 'Half-time!' she said.

The girls crowded round her, and she gave some general advice, then spoke to one or two by themselves. Then she came to Monica. 'You'd be good, you know,' she said, 'if you passed more. You're a bit—selfish, now. I'm going to put you in the centre for this half. A centre-forward's duty is to feed her wings and inners. I want you to practise doing that; never to keep the ball yourself at all. See?'

Monica nodded. It all fitted in with Francesca's theories. She had been playing to enjoy herself. Now she had got to play for the good of the forward-line.

Erica had planted her broad back between Monica and the crowd. 'And, Monica,' she said, low, so that the others could not hear, 'we don't swear, *ever*, on the field. See?'

Monica flushed. For a second she felt angry. Then she realised how Erica had shielded her, and a rush of loyalty to the big captain came over her. Fancy being so thoughtful for the feelings of a little worm like herself! 'I won't, any more,' she promised solemnly.

Erica smiled. And Monica felt that she had, in some way that she did not quite understand, made another friend.

She played carefully for the rest of the game. She found that centre-forward suited her splendidly. Her size and strength were useful, and she discovered that there was as much joy in pushing the ball round a grabbing opponent for an inner to pounce on, as in rushing along with it herself. Erica nodded approval at her once or twice, and she felt mightily rewarded.

* * * * * *

The rest of the term seemed to fly. Hockey gave Monica something to think about and to talk about to the other girls.

She was not put into any team, but several times she played as substitute in the team games, and vowed to get into one next season.

All her spare time she spent with Francesca. That small person talked to her, sometimes wisely, sometimes so idiotically that Monica was reduced to helpless giggles, and could not stop laughing even when she went to bed. She, told Monica all about her beloved St Francis—his hatred of dishonesty and ostentation, his refusal of riches or even comfort, his turning of the smallest talents to account in the service of his leader, even of laughter and contortions—if he did nothing but tumble grotesquely head-over-heels he did it in his leader's name; and, most of all, of his queer, childlike friendliness for every one, regardless of position or character; a friendliness which extended even to sun and moon—his mother and sister he called them—to fire and water, and to the birds and the animals, who came to him as to a magician. Francesca was very like him, Monica thought; the prefects, the gardener, the other girls in her form, the sheep-dog pup who had recovered and who followed her everywhere, were all alike to her, all treated with the same bubbling courtesy, all taken for granted as friends. The two of them pored over Chesterton's life of the saint, and decided with great solemnity to make the school their object of service, and to do everything they did to its honour.

'We'll have to be awfully careful,' Francesca said, 'to do everything as well as ever we can, and not to do anything beastly!'

'What'll happen if we forget?' Monica asked, her old obedience to force and force alone coming back to her.

'Happen? Oh, nothing; because nobody'll know. But *we* shall know. And we shall feel—oh, perfect creepy-crankies!'

'I s'pose we shall,' Monica doubtfully agreed. Now that

her mind was occupied in her leisure hours, Monica's work improved by leaps and bounds. She loved it even more, now that she had only a limited time to give to it, and worked furiously. Then there were the holidays to look forward to. The spring was coming and the holiday feeling was in the air. Francesca, after some mysterious hints and evasions, had produced a letter from her mother inviting Monica to spend a fortnight of the month at Cambridge; and Monica's parents, wonderfully, had consulted at once to the plan. So, what with the full present and the exciting future, Monica's second half-term seemed to her to be only about a quarter as long as the first had been.

CHAPTER IX.

REAL PEOPLE.

'WE'RE nearly there,' Francesca said from the window. 'That was Great Shelford. We'll be there in a minute.'

Monica withdrew her gaze from the green marshland, and crossed to Francesca's side of the carriage and peered out.

'It's no good doing that,' Francesca discouraged. 'You can't see a thing of the town from the train. People always try to.'

Monica wandered back again. As they chugged into Cambridge station she began to squeak. 'We're not goin' to stop! Look, *really* we're not, Robin!'

Francesca, christened so because of some far-away allusion to St Francis's birds, and because she looked so like a robin, hopping perkily on her thin legs, snorted: 'We are. It's a long station, that's all. Down trains all go to the top end of it.'

'An' look at those horses on the lines! What are they doing?'

'Draggin' trucks about,' Francesca replied. 'They always do it. Come on, we've stopped.' She stumbled out of the train and fell upon a lady who was standing there. A comfortable, kind-faced lady she was, shabbily dressed in gray; more shabbily than her own mother, Monica thought, as she stood and watched them.

The visitor was pulled forward and introduced, and at once surrendered to the lady's charming Cambridge voice and the kind look in her big gray eyes. She wasn't going to be any more afraid of Francesca's mother than of Francesca herself. A shabby, ramshackle Ford was waiting for them, and they rattled off, first along a wide road of shops and houses, then into the heart of the town, where the streets were narrow and college buildings appeared intermingled with the shops.

'It's the vac.,' Francesca told her, 'so the town's pretty empty.'

Monica wondered whatever it was like when it was full.

Then they swung out into the Madingley Road, over little flintstones that glittered as they were crushed under the wheels; and stopped at last, outside a low house with a russet roof, a long strip of pale lawn in front of it, spotted with crocuses and edged with waving daffodils.

Monica drew a little breath of delight. It was just such a house as she had always wanted.

'Tumble out,' Francesca's mother ordered, 'and I'll take Jerusha round to the back.'

They tumbled, and Francesca led the way up the red brick path.

'Who's Jerusha?' Monica asked.

'Jerusha? Oh!' Francesca broke into giggles. 'Only the car. Horrid old thing!'

Then Monica was struck dumb again by the sight of the trim maid who beamed on them, and the dark hall in which the only points of light seemed to come from the polished brass and the flowers in bowls.

'Where are the boys?' Francesca demanded of the maid.

'They don't come till to-morrow, miss.'

'Oh, bother! One of father's mistakes again! He said they came a day *before* me. I might've known he meant a day after. He never knows the days things happen on,' she added to Monica.

Then the professor himself appeared—a little, clean-shaven, sandy-haired man, the image of Francesca. Francesca jumped at him and hugged him, and dragged him forward to meet Monica. His voice when he spoke was somehow like Francesca's too.

Presently they went upstairs; first up a wide staircase, past walls hung with queer swords and chain-mail, then by a narrow, crooked way that led to a wide landing at the top of the house, papered with pictures like a scrap-book's page.

'This is *our* landing,' Francesca said. 'These two are the boys' rooms. Mine's over there, and opposite is the one we put our friends in. Come and see mine.'

Francesca's was an attic. The sloping roof met the irregular floor at one side, and opened into two big dormer windows at right angles to each other. One of them looked westwards, over flat fields, the other opened above the garden. 'Tennis court out there,' Francesca said; 'we'll practise.'

But Monica was intent on the room; the low bed with a bright cover, facing the west window; the book-rest and reading lamp by it, showing that reading in bed was not considered a sin; the arm-chair, with a foot-stool in front of it until its owner should grow taller; the picture of St Francis and the birds; the photographs of Francesca's friends and relations, and dogs and cats; and the book-cases full of books.

'Like it?' asked Francesca.

'Rather!'

'Come and see yours, then.'

The room across the passage was like Francesca's, without, of course, Francesca's individuality. Its window looked westward, too, into the sunset over the flat fields and little trees. There are no more beautiful sunsets in the world than those seen from Cambridge.

'They'll bring up your bag in a minute. Oh, here it is. I'm allowed down to dinner now. I wasn't before I went to school. Let's change, quick, then I can show you things.'

So Monica was left alone. She stared out of the window. She padded about over the soft old carpet; she looked at the books in the book-rest by the bed, and fingered the shining bed-rail; and finally washed in hot water out of a polished copper jug, and changed her dress.

It was all so different from her own home; so luxurious, and yet so old and shabby and natural, as if it had all been for years and years just as it was now. She had a moment's panic. Would she know how to behave? Would she do things that they did not do, or say queer things, or not understand what they meant? That was what had happened to her at Greystones, with every one except Francesca, until she had learnt the wisdom of keeping quiet and doing as every one else did. She wouldn't be able to keep quiet here; she would have to talk and they would all listen. She wished she could go home, now, at once! How could she possibly bear a fortnight of these strange people whom she had never seen before?

Then Francesca skipped in, and hurried her downstairs and introduced her to three dogs and a family of very new kittens, so new that their eyes were only just open. The gong boomed through the house before the kittens had all been looked at and named, and Monica found herself in the dining-room, opposite Francesca, at a table of glimmering silver and glass lit by shaded candles.

The professor talked to her in Francesca's own way, asking her opinion now and then, treating her as an equal. Mrs Lucas turned to her sometimes, and sometimes Francesca's chatter enveloped them all, and the glasses seemed to tinkle in echo to their laughter. They all took her quite for granted. She was a Greystones girl, and Francesca's friend.

After dinner the two girls sat on the floor in the library and played with the dogs, while the professor and Mrs Lucas drank coffee. They all talked, and the time flew by until about nine, when Mrs Lucas suggested bed. 'We're early folk,' she said. 'Perhaps you won't mind. Francesca likes to read for a little while, and then one of us comes up and turns out her light.'

So they went up again to the attic bed-rooms.

'Do they know—about me?' Monica asked her friend, as they undressed with their doors wide open and chattered to each other across the passage.

'What about you?'

'That I'm—different?'

'You *aren't* different. You're silly.'

'But do they know?' she persisted.

'They know you came to Greystones from an elementary school, if that's what you're gettin' at. Mother asked me what your father did, and I told her. And they know you're awfully clever, an' that you helped me find the pup, and got me down off that beam, and I think mother wrote to your mother to ask her to let you come. That enough?'

Monica heaved a sigh of great relief. 'I'm jolly glad they know,' she said.

'I think they like you,' Francesca said cheerfully, backing into her own room. 'They look as if they do. You ready for your bath? I'll show you where the bathroom is.'

Then came a long, exquisitely-comfortable night between cool sheets that smelt of lavender, an awakening to the fragrance of coffee and bacon, and breakfast under Mrs Lucas' kindly eye and the professor's mild chaff. Monica remembered anxiously having heard her father say something about the 'seven vulgar ways of eating an egg,' and watched Francesca covertly to see if she ate hers differently at home from at school. She did not appear to, and Monica plunged into her own with a healthy appetite.

After breakfast she ran with Francesca in the damp, sweet-smelling garden; then they packed themselves into the Ford and went with the professor into Cambridge to explore.

They wandered round and through the colleges, and Monica was speechless before the quaint courts of Queen's, the smooth lawns and tall corners and square, beautiful buildings of King's; the clear blue and crimson lights in the chapels; the warm pink of the stone in Trinity library; the vast kitchens and little tucked-away stairs.

Then, after lunch, Francesca's two brothers arrived, and the holiday really began.

CHAPTER X.

NEW EXPERIENCES.

JIM was older than Francesca, and Jerry younger. They took to Monica at once, and she to them. On the very night of their arrival the four of them made the attic floor resound with the challenging yells of a pillow fight. In the morning they played tennis, and Monica found to her joy that her play was quite up to their standard. She played more like a boy than a girl, with a strong overhand service and long, low strokes. She was a little bit slow, but that was compensated for by her strength. By the end of three sets, when they all staggered indoors with linked arms, she felt as if she had known the jolly, friendly family for years and years.

'No time to do an awful lot this afternoon, is there?' Jim, who was the leader of the revels, said at lunch-time.

'I should think you're too tired for much,' Mrs Lucas said, eyeing them benevolently as she spooned out big helpings of pudding.

'Tired? Oh, dear me, no!' they all protested.

'I know!' Jim looked across at his sister for approval. 'We'll take a punt on the Backs and teach young Monica how to pole. May we, mother?'

'Can Monica swim?' Mrs Lucas demurred.

'Oh yes! With my clothes on and all!' Monica told her eagerly.

'That's all right. It's pretty difficult to upset a punt, and if you fall out you can always get to it and hang on. Want your tea to take with you?'

What a perfectly amazing parent, Monica thought. Not only did she let her family adventure itself on the river alone, but she did not seem at all perturbed at the notion of their falling into the water so long as they managed to get out again.

Mrs Lucas seemed to read her thought, and turned to her with a smile. 'We all live on the river in the summer,' she said. 'The children could paddle canoes when they were six, and they're all quite capable of life-saving you if you should get stuck. I only make one rule—' She glanced round, and the family seemed completely taken up with the food on their plates and took no notice of her at all. So she went on, her eyes twinkling, 'that two changes of garments be taken with them, in case of accidents, if they're going farther than the Backs. That won't apply to-day, you see; you can come straight home if you get drowned.'

'Do you take boys' clothes, or girls'?' Monica inquired.

'A set of each. Francesca and Jerry are the worst culprits. But I have known Jerry and Jim to do it, and then Jerry has to come home in Francesca's clothes.'

The family broke out into giggles at that. Only Jim grumbled that it was a rotten plan, and didn't mother think they were old enough to give it up. Mrs Lucas looked detached. 'It's a rule, my son,' she said. 'You're never too old to get pneumonia, and if you did get it I should have the job of nursing you.' So Jim subsided, laughing.

They bicycled to the boathouse tucked under the bridge. The boatmen knew them, and hooked out a punt at once.

'That's the one,' Jerry approved. 'She's jolly and light, and yet she's solid. I know.'

Jim chortled malevolently at his junior's wisdom. They pitched cushions in, planted the bags of food in the middle, and arranged themselves with rugs. The sun was very hot, but there was still a tang in the wind.

Jim scorned paddles, and, taking the long pole from the boatman, swung them round with lordly ease and took them along with a prod, and a long, slow push which made the water gurgle round the punt's square nose.

'I'm not getting wet a *bit*,' he said proudly.

'You've improved, I think.' Francesca watched him with a critical eye. 'Yes, you're really jolly good now.'

'Thanks, awfully,' Jim grinned. 'Want it yourself, or what's the matter?'

'Thank you, yes.' Francesca hopped lightly up beside him and he handed her the pole and wriggled past her on to the cushions.

Francesca was just as capable as her brother. She looked like some tiny, graceful fairy, the sun shining through her yellow-red hair and the water dripping from her hand as she swung it off the pole and down to her side at the end of each stroke. Monica was entranced with her, and with the smooth green banks, the daffodils waving by John's stream, the gray willows over which a veil of delicate green was creeping, the bridges, the rosy, ivy-covered walls.

'My turn!' Jerry shouted presently.

'You be careful,' Jim warned him. 'Keep in the middle, and for any sake if you get stuck in the mud let the pole go. Get along.'

Jerry's progress was slow. He was not so strong as the others, and the pole was apt to wabble as he thrust it in, and to splash in the water as he threw it up for the next stroke. Still, he took them along straight in the middle of the stream and showed not the slightest concern when another punt slid very close by them.

They passed the austere walls of Queen's and crossed the pool into which the weir splashes from the upper river. Jim took them up one of the narrow side-streams to the mill, past houses with gardens which run down to the water; but the stream grew so shallow that they had to turn back for fear of sticking on the gravelly bottom. When they had passed the weir again, Francesca turned to Monica. 'You try, now!' she said. 'The current's with us—it's easier.'

'It looks easy,' Monica said unwisely, as she stepped cautiously along the boat.

Jerry sniggered wickedly, and Francesca said, 'You wait and see.'

Jim talked learnedly to her about what to do with the pole when she wanted this or that to happen, and she began to think that punting was perhaps not quite so simple after all.

She took the pole and dropped it gingerly into the water. It floated up behind her and nothing happened at all.

'*Push* it in!' Jim encouraged. 'Prod like anything!'

So Monica prodded, and the punt swung slowly round and butted its nose into the bank. 'Good thing there's not much traffic,' Jim said placidly.

'Don't get jolted off when she hits!' Francesca warned. 'There we are. *Now*, what are you goin' to do?'

Monica, balancing the pole horizontally, poked at the bank with it, and the punt moved round again and settled down alongside as though it meant to stay the night there. She pushed against the bank again but could not make the monster move. She remembered Jim's words about a perpendicular pole, and dropped the iron end deep into the mud; and the punt would do nothing but heave portentously round in circles, first one way and then the other. Each new movement brought muffled squeals of laughter from the three in the bottom. Francesca was rolled up in a ball in the middle, convulsed and tearful; Jerry, flat on his face, hooted at the top of his voice; and Jim watched her and just chuckled good-humouredly. They did not seem to mind in the least being stuck and unable to move except into the bank and out again. After about the tenth whirl, Monica was so weak with laughter that she could not do another thing. Generally she hated making a laughing-stock of herself, and got cross at once if she could not do what she wanted to do; but these people seemed so thoroughly to enjoy her ridiculous efforts, and to take her failure so much as a matter of course, that she felt that success would have been somehow unnatural, and was as amused as they were. She just stood there and laughed and drifted.

'I see why you were stuck up with not getting wet,' she told Jim. 'I'm simply drenched all down this side!'

'Of course you are,' Jim said. 'Every one is at first. It's only jolly good people who don't get wet, I can tell you. Look here, I'll come up there with you and we'll see what we can do.'

He stood over her, and shouted advice in her ear, and seized the pole and directed its end this way and that, and between them they kept quite creditably to the punt-path and hardly wabbled round at all. 'You have a rest now,' he said after a time. 'I'll just take her under the willow here, and we'll have tea.'

Monica's wet arm had been quite dried by the sun. She wrapped herself up in a rug like an Indian, and they sat in the punt and ate sandwiches and buns, and drank tea out of mugs, and the Lucases told stories of what the Backs were like in term, crammed with boats and noisy in the evenings with gramophones.

Then they practised with the pole again, and finally took the punt back to the landing-stage and bicycled home. After dinner they played riotous hide-and-seek in the rambling old house, and Monica slept like a top again between her sweet-smelling sheets.

CHAPTER XI.

TWO DAYS.

THE next morning they played tennis, and in the afternoon went a long ride on their bicycles. The day after, tennis again, and the professor and Mrs Lucas joined them in row-boats on the lower river, and Monica began to learn to row. She found it much easier than punting, although she did turn nearly head-over-heels into the professor's chest after one prodigious 'crab.'

The following day was Sunday, and they all went to King's Chapel and listened to the organ and the choir, and watched the ruby and sapphire lights from the old glass in the windows. In the afternoon they had a walk, and in the evening just talked. The family treated each other as equals, just as they treated other people, and talked about all sorts of subjects with perfect frankness—religion and conduct, and how one felt when one was frightened, and how just being frightened did not make one a coward, and heaps of other things that Monica could not remember afterwards. They did not do very much on that Sunday, but it stayed in Monica's head as one of the happiest days she had ever spent. It was so quiet and peaceful, and full of companions who liked her, and the professor's talk was so wise and so funny.

The rest of the week flew by very happily. She and Francesca practised tennis with great keenness; they had by no means forgotten their ambition to be famous. They made a formidable pair when they played together. Very often they beat the boys, for Monica was so steady and sure, and Francesca so quick and surprising and wily. Monica did a certain amount of solid reading, too, and Francesca whirled off some excellent sketches of her and of the boys.

Two days stood out particularly clearly to Monica when she looked back on the holiday. There was much of it which she remembered, of course—learning to row and to paddle a canoe, and to set off gleefully on one's wild lone in a 'Rob Roy,' with paddles flapping on each side like a water-boatman's legs; the wild games with the boys; and the clever, clear-cut, kindly talk of the Lucas family. But these two days stayed in her memory with their outlines all unblurred.

The first was a day on the river. They started off in a punt in the morning, up the Granta towards Grantchester. They took turns to punt, rounding the corner by Newnham swimming-bath in great style, and sweeping round fallen trees that Jim, the river-wise, warned them about long before they could be seen. Then they saw a king-fisher. That was the first wonderful thing. It flashed across the sunny river like an arrow of shimmering, electric blue, turned for an instant to show them its waistcoat of pink and gray, and was gone. Monica's heart stood quite still. She had never seen anything so startlingly beautiful. In a few minutes they came to the orchard, and climbed out to have lunch. The apple-blossom was out, and they sat among the gray trunks of the trees, in a fairy bower of pink and white, breathing the blossom's wonderful honey smell. Monica thought it was even more lovely than the king-fisher, so quiet and delicate and sweet. They went on again, turning to the left at the fork to reach Byron's Pool, creeping up among the trees. At the pool they had their work cut out, even the four of them pulling and pushing all together, to get the punt over the weir. They took off their shoes and stockings and waded, and rolled up their sleeves and heaved up the steep, muddy bank; and presently the punt floated in the wide, clear stretch above the pool, and they climbed into her and rested in the sun.

Jerry took the pole. He turned them round and started them efficiently enough, then plunged the pole in. 'It's muddy,' he said. He pushed them along for several strokes, slowly. Then the catastrophe happened. He prodded the muddy bottom as usual—and the pole stuck fast.

'Turn it, gumpy!' Jim grunted.

Jerry wriggled and twisted; and the punt, reacting to the push on the pole, glided on.

'Let go!' Francesca and Jim shrieked together.

But Jerry couldn't. He clung tight to the pole, and clawed at the punt with his feet. He pushed his tip-toes into one of the ridges in the boards and pulled. But it was no good. The punt floated on, and Jerry stayed with the pole. At first it was upright, and he clung like a monkey; then it heeled slowly, slowly over with his weight, and with a splash Jerry flopped in, still clinging.

Monica was horrified; but the other two were spluttering with laughter.

'Hold on to it, you old ass!' Jim shouted.

Jerry, whose face had not gone under, grinned wanly, 'It's jolly cold!' he remarked in resigned tones. 'I'm goin' to swim!'

Francesca and Jim had the paddles out in a twinkling, and were backing the punt towards him.

'There's another one in the bottom,' Jim told Monica. 'You help!'

Monica did. But she kept a puzzled eye on Jerry. 'He's swimming *away* from us!' she said in a minute. 'Or am I dotty?'

'It's the current!' Francesca looked anxious for a second. 'He's pulled the pole out of the mud with his swimming, and it's carrying him down!'

Monica felt herself go white. 'The weir!' she whispered. She put down her paddle and began to kick off her shoes.

Jim saw her out the corner of his eye. 'Don't do that! Paddle!' he commanded. 'The current's helping us. It 'ud hinder you if you tried to swim; you'd never get back. Paddle like blazes!'

They had suddenly turned very solemn. They paddled as hard as ever they could, Jim on one side, Monica and Francesca on the other. And they gained. They drew gradually nearer to the little fair head by the floating pole. Their arms ached as though they would drop off. But they drew level, and Monica stretched out a long arm and grabbed the end of the pole. Jerry came along it hand over hand, still grinning, and climbed in.

Instantly the Lucases were themselves again, scuffling out of his way as he dripped over them, calling him and each other names.

'You loon! Why didn't you leave go?'

'Couldn't. Hands got stuck, somehow.'

'You did look funny! Monkey on a stick wasn't in it!'

'Felt funny, too! The water just seemed to rise up gradually. It wasn't a bit like falling in.'

Francesca had been burrowing in one of the bags. 'Here you are!' she said, throwing a bundle at him. So the small boy changed his clothes right down to his skin, and rubbed himself dry on the cushions, as placidly as if he did it every day.

'Votes we have tea,' Jim said when that was done.

Jerry agreed. 'My bathe's made me hungry,' he said.

So they had tea among the rushes by the bank. And as they floated down again on the way home, the fourth incident happened.

They were not paddling, just floating with the stream, a paddle stuck out behind to keep them straight. Monica saw it first—a little gray head the size of a walnut, with great eyes rimmed with gold. 'It's—it's a goblin!' she said, almost under her breath.

It was floating along, a little slower than they were going themselves. Its arms were folded over its chest, its long legs out behind it kicked widely now and then in a vigorous stroke.

'It's a goblin, swimming!'

It half closed its big eyes. It seemed wrapped in lazy content.

They all crowded to the side of the punt to look at it, talking in whispers lest they should frighten it. Then suddenly it gathered its legs up under it and leapt straight into Monica's green linen lap.

'Oh—oh!'

They all stared down at it wonder-struck.

Then they broke into chuckles.

'It's a toad! An old gran'-dad toad!' Jerry chortled.

It sat placidly watching them. Perhaps it thought Monica's green dress was a water-lily leaf. Then it leapt off into the sunlit air, and plop into the water, kicked once or twice, and was still again. They saw it floating behind them, its little square head out of the water, its eyes half shut.

* * * * * *

That day it was which awoke something in Monica which had never been awake before. It was as if Cambridge had laid a gentle, moss-covered hand on her and had shown her what beauty was; had given her some of its own quiet, kindly self-sufficiency, its peace that came from some store of beauty inside itself, and never failed, however it was buffeted by life outside. Many people do not get it until they have spent three years in one of the colleges and are about to come down. To Monica, perhaps because she had fewer advantages than most of the girls who come to Newnham and Girton, it came earlier and penetrated more quickly. But after that day she was never quite the same Monica. She moved more quietly and serenely, and minded less what other people thought of her, though more what she thought of herself. She was honest with herself before that holiday. In the Lucases she found companions who were honest with other people too; who knew instinctively what people were in spite of what they seemed to be; who went through life with the minimum of prejudice to deceive them. The contact with them helped her to understand the other girls at Greystones, while it did not blind her, as the influence of slightly different people might have done, to the goodness which her own family possessed and the Greystones girls, as a class, did not. She realised that her own people had disadvantages; but she did not despise them—she only vowed to lift them, if she could, out of some of the squalor and preoccupation with material things which are inseparable from poverty and hard work.

The other great day helped to show her how the lifting might be done.

The party had played tennis, as usual when nothing more exciting was going on, all the morning. After lunch they wandered across the road into the woods there, with no purpose but to be out in the sweet-smelling sunshine.

They rambled on, talking and chaffing, uncovering a violet here, a primrose there, now and then an early oxlip, and so to a path and a gate. At the gate they stopped and sniffed the air.

'Cowslips!' Francesca shouted, skipping and clapping her hands.

The field was edged with big trees—oaks, just coming out into tiny knotted catkins—and fell away in a bank below them. The bank was covered with golden, nodding heads, so close one could not step between them; and from them floated up the sour-sweet, intoxicating smell which cowslips have and primroses faintly echo.

They tumbled over the gate in a flurry and flung themselves on the grass below the bank, where the flowers were more scanty. They picked handfuls, all they could carry, without leaving a trace behind them, so crowded were the flowers, and sat down again to tie the bunches up with grass.

'We'll go on, straight across, shall we?' Francesca said. 'It's lovely here.'

It was lovely. The flat green fields seemed to stretch for miles, cut by low hedges over which blackthorn in flower cast a fairy spray, dotted with flat-topped maple-trees whose shiny, yellow-green leaves were bursting from red buds, and here and there a crab-apple in bloom. Sometimes there were streams by the hedges, with little muddy bridges over them where the gates gave access. Some of the fields were drained with parallel ditches, which had to be leapt. In some there were herds of young cattle, which gathered silently round them, necks stretched in curiosity, when they sat down to rest, and fled galumphing, tails in the air, when they moved on again. In others there were big shire horses with little foals beside them wabbling on long legs. One of the foals let them come quite close to it and see the queer bristling beard sticking out from its velvet under-lip. But when they tried to stroke it, it frisked back to its mother.

'Aren't we trespassing?' Monica asked once, as they passed from field to field.

'Oh no. At least, the farmers don't mind so long as we shut the gates. Let's vault this one; it's a high one. You first, Robin.'

Francesca flung herself at it, poised herself a second on her hands with legs straight up, close together, and dropped lightly over.

'Oh, lovely! How do you do it?' Monica gasped.

'It's easy as winks! Look!'

The boys showed her, and Jim came back to tell her where

to put her hands. She rolled over, very clumsily it seemed to her, though Jim and Jerry assured her it was 'jolly good for a beginner.' Then they must all go back again to practise, until they were tired of it, and Monica's legs at her last attempt were as vertical as Francesca's had been.

'It's a jolly good way of getting over,' Francesca said. 'Doesn't show your petticoats, even if you're grown up and have long ones, if you do it properly. It's because you go so quick. Mother does it sometimes.'

'You face the way you're going when you come down, too,' Jim said. 'That's jolly important in a paper-chase. You don't lose any time.'

They wandered on. To Monica the freedom was amazing. All those wide fields to do as they liked in, without fear of any one so long as they did no damage! No notice-boards, such as she ran against in her rare expeditions from Enford into Epping Forest, warning her not to do this or that; no orange-peel and papers; no suspicious keepers; no crowds of rowdy boys; no smelly motor-buses; and over all, the quiet, smiling happiness of Cambridge.

'Where are we?' she asked.

'Getting on towards the Huntingdon Road, I should think,' Jerry said. 'Yes; there's the windmill that draws up the water, and there's Girton Tower.'

'Let's go and see Miss Bayliss,' Francesca suggested. 'She'd love some cowslips!'

'Aren't we too dirty?' Jim demurred.

They looked down at themselves.

'Don't think so,' Francesca decided. 'We're only a bit muddy about the legs. She doesn't mind dirt, either. She likes gardening.'

'Right-o! Hope she's at home.'

'Who is she?' Monica asked as they set off in a line for the little round windmill.

'Mistress of Girton,' Francesca explained. 'Great friend of ours. Most people are frightened of her, but we're not.'

Monica privately thought that she might be. But she followed the others and said nothing.

They walked through the farm buildings and came out to the straight white road.

'We'll go in the front way,' Francesca said, 'because Monica hasn't seen it.'

So they came decorously up the drive between the evergreens, feeling very little as the great square red tower loomed over them. Under the archway that pierced it, they stopped.

'You find out whether she's in, Robin,' Jim directed. 'You're cleanest.'

They saw her talking to the rosy little portress, then she beckoned to them and they all stepped into the red stone hall.

Francesca appeared to know the place very well. She led them along for a few steps, then seemed to dive into the wall; and they clambered up a tiny spiral staircase of white stone on to the landing above, crossed a wide corridor, and stopped outside a door at the end of a little passage.

'Come in!' they heard.

Then Monica found herself following them across a soft carpet to an arm-chair in the very far distance, where a lady sat by the open window. She rose to meet them, and Monica thought she had never seen any one so tall and thin and grim. The graying hair was drawn back from a face that was almost a skeleton, high cheek-bones supporting a thin nose that beaked over a straight line of mouth. She felt a sudden sympathy with the people who were afraid of Miss Bayliss. Then the apparition smiled. The straight lips parted and curled upwards, making clefts in the cheeks. The eyes revealed themselves of startling twinkling blue between networks of wrinkles.

'Hullo,' Miss Bayliss said easily. 'Hullo, ragamuffins!'

Francesca leapt upon her, and she caught the grubby little figure up and kissed her. The boys hugged her too, with no trace of self-consciousness. She came forward and held out a hand to Monica, the other deep in Francesca's mop. Monica shyly met the blue eyes, and felt her hand clasped strongly. The Lucases began to talk, all at once, and Monica had time to look round the room. The wall was crowded with pictures—all sorts of pictures—water-colours, medieval prints, Greek gods and temples; queer, foreign-looking oddments stood on bookshelves and tables; of furniture there was not much in spite of the room's great size, but what was there was very lovely and very comfortable. The room was quiet yet full of colour, luxurious and yet austere, harmonious and yet intensely personal. Then she was drawn into the conversation too, into reminiscences of the holiday, stories of Greystones. Miss Bayliss had the quality of treating them all as equals; and yet she seemed to tower above them, surveying them wisely with her kind blue eyes.

'What were you doing,' Jerry inquired, 'when we came in?'

Miss Bayliss stretched out a hand towards a pile of paper on the floor. 'Writing.'

''Nother book?' Jerry persisted.

She nodded. 'Yes.'

'Shall we like it? Is it like the last one?'

'It's rather learned,' she told him gravely. 'History.'

He looked disappointed. So she changed the subject. 'Will you stay and have tea with me?'

'May we?' they eagerly asked.

'I wish you would. I'm all by myself with no one to talk to.'

'Then we will, please.'

Miss Bayliss crossed the room to the bell. Many people would have asked one of the children to ring it. She treated them as politely as she would have any other visitor, however grown-up and grand. And presently a solidly luscious tea came in—bread and butter and honey, plum cake and chocolate biscuits. When they had finished, Francesca stood up. 'May I show Monica round?' she said. 'She's never been up before.'

Miss Bayliss turned to Monica with a smile. 'You should have come in term-time,' she said. 'It's much more exciting. But go round, by all means.'

Francesca and Monica explored the long corridors. They went into some of the students' rooms—little square sitting-rooms with bedrooms communicating with them, big windows opening on to lawns or rough grass-land with clumps of pines.

'Two of these all to one's self?' Monica asked in amazement.

'Yes. You're given them when you come up, and you can move once while you're here to anywhere else you like.'

'And no one can come in unless you let them?'

'No. They always have to knock. And you can put up a notice to say you don't want any one if you like.'

They went into the great bleak hall with its long tables and its portraits of pioneers; into the little warm laboratory on the edge of the tennis courts; into the reception-rooms where one could hold parties; the lecture-rooms and the big, quiet library; and the changing-rooms, full of racks of hockey-sticks and shoes and pads; then back to Miss Bayliss, a quick good-bye, and home, by the road this time.

'And in term-time a girl lives in every one of those rooms?'

'Yes,' said Francesca. 'Of course.'

'And goes to lectures and works in that lab, and otherwise does just as she likes?' Monica went on.

'Yes, within limits. Has to be in by ten, and things like that.'

'An' Miss Bayliss is over them all?'

'Yes. There are lots of other dons, of course; but she's the mistress. Principal, they call it at Newnham.'

'I like "mistress" best,' said Monica firmly. She added straightway to her store of vows. She would win a scholarship to Girton and to nowhere else; she would have a room in the old wing on the middle floor; and presently she would be a don and write books.

* * * * * *

She had a fortnight at home, revelling in the interest her family took in her stories; shopping and doing housework with her mother just for the pleasure of being with her to talk to her; listening to her father's quaint wisdom in the evenings, enjoying his half-amused pride in her and her high ambitions. She had always been something of an idol at home, but she had been brought up too sensibly to be spoiled. It was just that her father and mother saw in her what they would have wished to be themselves, and determined that she should have the chances which had been denied them.

Then the holidays were over, and it was time to go back to school; to Greystones, with its crowd of suspicious companions and pernickety prefects; and to Francesca.

CHAPTER XII.

TENNIS TIES.

AT Greystones they met like old friends.

'Hullo, old thing!' Francesca grinned, on her knees by her locker.

'Hullo, Robin! Did you go to the Orchard again?'

'No; but Jerry fell out of his "Rob Roy"—' And they were off, deep in holiday chatter, which lasted them all through supper and until bed-time.

Monica was a little bit chastened to find that the girls were not as friendly to her as she felt towards them. She was actually glad to come back. She would not have believed it possible last term. And, if they did not seem as warm to her as she would have liked, they were very much warmer than last term, when she had been left right outside all the talk and laughter.

So she comforted herself, as she packed books into her desk in the Lower Fifth classroom. And then the amazing thing that she had been wishing for hopelessly all through the holiday happened. The form-room door opened and Francesca staggered in, panting under her load of books. 'I've been moved up!' she proudly announced.

'Robin! Really and truly?'

''Course! D'you think I should be plunging in here for any other reason? Show me where I can have a desk!'

After some conferring and a little haggling, the two were installed side by side.

'Can't think why they did it!' Francesca chattered. 'I was top in Latin and algebra and geometry, of course, and English was just Shakespeare that I couldn't help knowing about. But I *was* surprised! Isn't it just topping?'

Monica was looking straight in front of her lest she should devour Francesca with her eyes. Lesson-time last term had been a little private purgatory to her, to be borne because it led to other times when Francesca was there to talk to. Now it was going to be—just heavenly!

They were always together after that. And the other girls in their form, because they were no longer solitary, and because they began to be known to be clever and were obviously unassuming, started to take an interest in them. They were no longer left out of conversations—not that Francesca ever had been, but Monica had, always, in the Lower Fifth—and joined in naturally and without effort, Monica following Francesca's lead at first, but gradually learning to stand on her own feet in this as in other matters. The girls received her remarks in silence at first; then, after turning them over in their minds, found them sensible and not to be despised, and admitted her without further to-do into their counsels. Francesca took a tremendous interest in the life of the form, its societies, its gossip, its reputation generally; and Monica began to do the same, and to contribute her own share of knowledge and ideas to it. She was beginning, only half-consciously, to give. Almost at once she learned the joy of taking, from the form's ready loyalty and appreciation.

The form talked about them, quite a lot, among its own members. Francesca was such a queer little person. She had to be explained.

'She's conceited!' some of them said, seeing her talking to the veterans of the Lower Fifth as if she had known them all her life.

'No—not conceited. Look!' some one would object, as Francesca trotted off at tea-time to wait on some girl scarcely her senior, or cleaned the dusty blackboard with all the humility proper to the newest member of the form.

'She's affected!' The first would change her ground, watching the thin little figure skipping and snapping its fingers by Monica's side. 'Showing off to Monica Baxter, who doesn't know a hopeless ass when she sees one!'

Then they would see the form prefect, or some one equally important, doubling up in chuckles before Francesca's wit, and a bark of laughter would tell of a whimsical comment from the generally silent Monica, to round off the tale; and they would join the group and swell the laughter, and go away agreeing that Francesca was frightfully funny and Monica not so bad after all.

It was tennis, as they had hoped, which brought the pair conclusively into the lime-light. They seized upon empty courts and practised unobtrusively whenever they could, and quietly one day added their names to the list of those wishing to enter for the Junior (under sixteen) House Championships.

Erica, with a watchful eye for people who should think they were better than they really were and enlarge the list unnecessarily with 'rabbits,' watched them from a window as they practised, and went away with a twinkle in her eye, wondering whether some other people's noses would not be wrenched speedily out of joint.

The Lower Fifth eyed the lists nonchalantly. 'Junior champions? Oh, Mildred and Jean, of course. Every one else'll be out of it double quick against those two. 'Fraid we sha'n't win the School Championship with them, though.'

Then the ties were drawn.

'Who's Mildred playing in the first round? Inez, from the Fourth Remove, isn't it? And Jean? Oh, fat Marjorie. They'll win every game against those two.'

The House trooped off to watch these two games; and Monica and Francesca, with satisfied winks—for they did not want to be watched thus early and be put off their game—went off to play their own first rounds. They had been very much afraid that they might meet each other in the early rounds and spoil each other's chances. But by great good luck they were in different halves of the draw from the very first, and would not meet—if at all—before the finals.

Monica's opponent was a girl from the Upper Fifth, who could have been a really good player if she had not been so anxious to show off. She treated Monica with disdain, and smashed down a raking, ragged service which wriggled along the court and bounced away at an angle. Monica missed the first two completely by standing too near the net. But for the third service she stood back, and astonished Audrey, her rival, with a long, low shot to the back-line. Audrey was so surprised that she served double faults for the rest of the game.

The honours were easily with Monica as soon as she had sized her opponent up. Sometimes Audrey's showy strokes succeeded, and then Monica lost a point; more often they landed in the net or among the trees behind the court; and if they were in any way possible to take, Monica took them and sent them back. Slow she might be, but she was very very sure, and it was a very superfine return that found her baffled. She disposed of Audrey with twelve games to three. The Greystones championships are settled, not by sets, which may drag on for a whole afternoon, but by playing fifteen games in each tie.

Monica strolled across to another court, where she found Francesca jigging up and down to the great discomfort of her adversary who was one who lobbed steadily and used her brains not at all.

The honours were easily with Monica.

'So that's that,' Francesca said contentedly as they marched away together.

'Twelve-three! That's a pretty good score!' the House said, reading the lists at the end of the day. 'And look here—thirteen-two, that little midget Francesca Lucas beat Faith Gordon! Faith must've been nervous, or something.'

Even after the next round, when Monica had, by steady application to business, defeated a much better rival than Audrey by eleven games to four, and Francesca had achieved the amazing total of fifteen-nil against some one who had drawn a bye, the House was not moved.

'They'll be lucky if they get two games between them against Mildred and Jean,' it was said.

After the third round the critics were a little less sure. Some of them had bestirred themselves to watch 'these new kids' playing.

'They really are pretty good,' they acknowledged. 'Wonder where they learnt to play? And wonder what Mildred and Jean'll make of them?' For the two had won their third rounds with considerable ease, and now they were both in the semi-finals against the favourites.

Mildred, who was Monica's opponent, was the more formidable of the two. She had been the second of Mason's Junior pair last year, and every one expected her to sail into the first place with no trouble at all, last year's first champion being now over sixteen and too old for the Junior games. Jean, the other 'probable,' had been considered good last year too.

Monica gasped as she walked out to the court to play that match. It seemed that the whole House was gathered to watch. Erica was there, and Evelyn and Penelope, and the games-mistress, and nasty, superior Mavis, and quite a number of people from other Houses also.

The semi-finals were, in a way, more important than the final. For the two finalists would probably be champions in any case, and play together for the House; the losers in the semi-finals were out of the championship entirely, unless one of them should challenge the finalist who had not beaten her and should win.

Mildred was a pleasant opponent. She was too good a player to think herself infallible, and she had watched Monica's play, and knew that she was going to have to fight to keep her laurels. But she smiled good-humouredly as they tossed for service and side, and was almost apologetic when she won the toss and chose the shady end of the court.

Monica had watched her opponent too, and knew quite a lot about her play; how, if her first, fast service did not come off, the second was always a lob for safety; how, although she *could* take back-handers, it was a matter of luck whether they came back over the net or not, and how, when they did come back, they were not accurately placed; and how she was very slow to move for anything that came straight at her.

But, in spite of this knowledge, Monica found to her disgust that she was nervous. Her first few services wobbled off her racquet. They were not faults; but they were very easy for Mildred to take and do what she liked with; and Mildred, more used to crowds of spectators, very efficiently did, and won the game amid a patter of hands.

Then Mildred served; and when Monica had tipped several fierce slashes quietly back again just out of Mildred's reach, she began to look round to see where she could most usefully place her shots. Her play was pretty to watch, long and low and leisured, with an occasional quick, hard stroke when an opportunity came. But she could not altogether get over that panic. She knew what she wanted to do, but her wrist just would not quite do it; and Mildred won that game too, and the next; and the fourth as well, after several 'deuces.' The watchers began to be a little bored. They shifted on their feet, and several of them strolled away.

'She's no good against a person with experience, you see,' some one said.

'Never thought she would be, really,' another replied.

But Monica, strangely, felt quite sure of herself. Through those four games the score had been creeping up in her favour. She could feel herself improving. The next game she would win. She did. She served three straight, swift shots, one to Mildred's right, the next to her left, where she was not expecting it, and the next, when Mildred was dancing on one leg waiting for it to come in the middle of the court, to her left again. Then Mildred toppled one just over the net and won a point; and the next she returned decisively towards the back-line; only, unfortunately for its author, Monica decided to volley it, met it midway, and pushed it to the very far right-hand corner, where Mildred could not get near it at all.

The crowd clapped good-humouredly. That game had been well won. The volley had been played at the right minute. They liked a player who could dole out a winning stroke just when the game demanded it. And Monica found herself with that stroke, and played carefully, brainily on. And presently the games were four-all.

'Shouldn't wonder if Mildred didn't get another game,' Monica heard Erica say, and thrilled to the praise.

She did. She got two more. But nine-six is quite a decisive victory of new over old, and the two games which Mildred did wrest from her were only won after several 'deuces,' and both won by short shots. So there was no question about the matter at all. Monica had won, and Mildred was a champion no longer, unless she should manage to beat the winner of the other semi-final. She showed herself a proper public-school girl in her reception of her defeat. She shook hands with Monica, and raced away hand in hand with her to put the score down on the notice-board. '*Topping* game!' she said enthusiastically. 'Wasn't it? I enjoyed it awfully all the time.'

Monica shyly agreed.

'P'r'aps I'll lick Jean, and we'll be champions together,' Mildred rattled on. 'I always *do* lick Jean. I don't think we'd make a frightfully good pair, as a matter of fact; do you? We play too much alike. We'd be deadly steady—oh, *deadly* steady; every one would hate playing against us.'

The possibility of Jean's succumbing to Francesca did not seem to enter her head, or any one else's either. One thrilling defeat was all they could take in for one afternoon.

But Jean did succumb, very early in the proceedings. Francesca danced to and fro, slashed at the net and scooped at the back-line, ran faster than any one could imagine possible, and volleyed when every one would have said the ball was higher than she could reach, and fast enough to knock her over. She won the first ten games without a break, and gave Jean the rest. And the next day she fought doggedly with Mildred and beat her too.

'Those two kids are champions, sure enough,' was Erica's opinion. 'I thought they would be when I first saw them play. And a jolly good pair they'll make. They've more go in them than any two juniors since I've been in Mason's.' Which was a very long time.

Then came the question of which of them was to be first champion.

'Does it matter?' Monica asked, when Erica told them to arrange the time for the match.

'Oh yes! It's always done. Senior one takes the toss, and all that! This afternoon at three, I think. There won't be much of a crowd, I expect; the excitement's over now.'

But a crowd there was, all the same. The pair of new girls had somehow tickled the House's fancy, now that they had been brought before its eye. They were such dark horses; no one had expected this brilliance of them; it was such very striking brilliance, too. And they were known to be friends, which increased the interest.

They came out together.

'Oh, this is all rot!' Francesca grunted. 'Here, heads or tails?'

Erica was tossing for them.

'Heads,' said Monica.

'It's tails; I'll serve,' Francesca gloated. 'I hate your great, low whizzy-bangs.'

Francesca still served underhand, but her delivery was swift, and had a curl in it which Monica never quite liked. It defeated Monica several times, and won the game for Francesca.

The same thing happened when Monica served. The whizz-bangs won the game; and so on until the score was three-all.

Then Francesca came to the net and beckoned. 'This is rotten,' she said. 'If we go on like this I shall win just because I won the toss and took service. It's not fair. We're just being most stupidly cautious, and it's dull. Let's just play as we do when we play for fun. It doesn't matter which of us wins, does it?'

Monica grinned at her. 'Right-o!' she said.

So they stopped being so horribly, solemnly cautious, and enjoyed themselves. Francesca sent strokes hustling straight for Monica's middle, and laughed when she jumped ponderously out of the way; Monica tempted Francesca up to the net and then sent a lob over her head or a low stroke a hair's breadth out of her reach on one side or the other. They stopped winning their own services so regularly; but presently the score stood at seven-all just the same.

Francesca served and Monica returned; Francesca whirled it swiftly to Monica's right, close to the ground; Monica blocked it with a half-volley which sailed out of Francesca's reach.

'Love-fifteen,' the umpire droned.

Francesca served again, and Monica's stroke swished along the left-hand line. Francesca managed a pretty back-hander, but Monica predicted shrewdly where that back-hander would fall, and sent it back again; not without difficulty, though, and to a place where Francesca could easily take it. Francesca did take it, and won the point. The next point Monica lost too, by being rather too strong and placing the ball just outside the back-line.

'Thirty-fifteen.'

Monica brought it up to thirty-all by a clever volley from the middle of the court. Francesca quickly countered by putting an untouchable twist on her next service.

'Forty-thirty.'

The serve after that Monica returned with all her might; instinctively she knew that Francesca would not be able to return it very strongly, and she raced up to the net to kill the lob as it came.

Into Francesca's eyes there flashed a wicked twinkle. She seized her racquet in both hands and scooped, blatantly and without shame, for all she was worth, and watched the ball soar over Monica's head. Then with a sunny smile that seemed to say 'That's finished it,' she turned her back and strolled away from the net. She was half-way to the back-line when she was startled by a roar from the spectators. Monica had rushed after the ball and had hit it, amazingly, over her shoulder. It bounced coyly on Francesca's left. She lashed out wildly, missed it, and threw back her head to join in the crowd's laughter.

'Deuce.'

It was quickly over then. Francesca, perhaps a little flustered by her miscalculation, served a double fault; and the next ball Monica returned, with a grin, straight at Francesca's feet. She jumped in instinctive self-defence. The ball sailed away to the wall behind, and the crowd broke up in confusion and laughter, leaving the umpire to announce that 'Games are eight-seven. Monica Baxter wins.'

Francesca was round the net in a twinkling. 'Hurrah, congrats.! Come in, quick, out of every one's way!'

They took hands and tore, helter-skelter, across the garden and into a bathroom.

'Ripping game,' Francesca said contentedly. 'The best we've had.'

'It seems rotten, though,' Monica objected, 'for me to lick you. It was your idea from the very beginning. I should never even have played without you.'

'An' now we'll be playing together in matches, and you can order me about and make me have which court you like!' Francesca grinned.

'I feel a pig!' Monica said.

Francesca plunged her whole face into the basin she had filled. 'Bor-burroo-bor-bor-a-boroo!' she remarked from the bottom. Then, lifting a purple and dripping countenance, 'That's all bishy-bosh!' she said.

CHAPTER XIII.

MISTAKES.

THE Lower Fifth received them with applause, and for the next few days Monica lived in Paradise. She had Francesca always by her side to follow, if she wished, in small points of speech and behaviour. The two were the heroes of their form and the talk of their House. Their juniors looked at them with admiration, their equals with respect; Upper Fifth Mildred took a fancy to them, and walked and talked with them; those three monarchs of the Sixth, Erica and Evelyn and Penelope, smiled at them and congratulated them; and they were invited to practise on the courts with the two pairs of Senior House champions, to improve their game for the series of ties in which the five Houses competed for the school cup.

It seemed to Monica that in a few days she had attained to everything she could want at Greystones. She had been something of a hero all her life. At home she was petted because she was the only girl, and because she was so clever and so ambitious; at school at Enford everything had combined to make her a leader—her size and strength, her striking colouring, her splendid brain, and, above all, a certain refinement of upbringing that her companions lacked. Admiration, though she did not yet realise it, was as necessary to her as oats to a race-horse. With it she was a meteor; without it, a cinder scarcely glowing. And at Greystones it had passed her by. All the qualities that had seemed so important at Enford had been at a discount. Now she had come to her own again, and she basked in the sunshine.

Then came a set-back. Looking back on it afterwards, Monica saw that it was inevitable. She had travelled too rapidly up the road to success—she could not help but stumble; and indeed if she had been successful all along the line she would not have become the splendid person she developed into later. She would have been hard, like a diamond. As it was, she learned sympathy as well as success.

The bad day started, as had bad days before, with Mavis. Mavis had never relented to her as had the rest of the House, had always held aloof. Monica had hardly noticed it; she had been too much taken up with other things.

Then she met Mavis, as usual, coming out of the bath-room, and Mavis paused in her dignified walk, looked Monica deliberately up and down, leisurely transferred her gaze to her own satin-embroidered dressing-gown and silk pyjamas, then back again to Monica, with a little sneer, and went on her way.

Monica's eyes had followed Mavis. When she had turned away, Monica looked at herself again. Her dressing-gown was of faded flannel. Once it had been deep purple; now it was a drab lilac, and not even the same tint all over. Her pyjamas were of some thin cotton stuff, faded too, and not very well made.

She flushed slowly, realising the contrast between the two of them. Mavis, sleek-haired even at that time of day; leisured; dressing-gown, pyjamas, and slippers all delicately matching each other. And Monica, with black, tousled hair and defiant eyes; dressing-gown lilac, pyjamas faded pink, and slippers of navy-blue felt, with glaring red insides; tidy, perhaps, except for the hair, but very very shabby; and a fighter, for work and not for show. She hated Mavis, hated her more than ever. It was not Monica's fault she was poor, any more than Mavis's riches were to her credit. Riches were nothing to be proud of. How could any one be so petty as to sneer at shabby clothes?

School uniform ensured that one was free of criticism by day; but Mavis—mean, superior Mavis—had found the Achilles' heel of the scholarship girl's equipment, and did not hesitate to wound that tender spot with her boring, piercing glance.

Monica flounced into the bath-room, out of temper with the whole universe. 'Sausage-face! Sausage-face! Sausage-face! *Sausage*-face!' she muttered to herself. It eased her feelings. She saw Mavis's yellow opulent-looking sponge left on the floor, and took a running kick at it. It soared out of the window. She did not bother to look where it had fallen. 'Poor sponge!' she said regretfully. 'It'll go mouldy. But it's *her* fault.'

She felt better after that, and when she met Mavis on her way to breakfast, passed her with a jaunty swish of her tail. But it was a pity the enmity between them had flared up again to spoil her enjoyment.

At break in the middle of the morning it was spoiled still further, and, what made the tragedy seem all the greater, it was spoiled by Francesca. Monica, racing into the garden, found Francesca squatting on the ground prodding something with a stick. 'It's a lovely one—a *splendid* one!' she was murmuring. Monica bent over her eagerly—then jumped back with a yell, and refused to approach within two yards again. For Francesca's find was jet black, nearly three inches long, with horny red-gold legs and jagged, waving antlers above its head.

'Oh Robin, don't—don't! It'll bite you, and you'll die!'

Francesca continued to wriggle her stick gently underneath the creature, who clung to it with his claws. 'They don't bite,' she grunted, intent on her task.

'Is it—is it a scorpion?' Monica quavered.

Francesca raised the stick with the insect hanging to it, and Monica hopped quickly farther away. Francesca looked at her directly for the first time, and let out a bark of laughter. 'Why, you're frightened! You old silly! No, it's only a stag-beetle. Come and look at him close.'

But Monica would not. She hated spiders, and beetles, and earwigs, and hairy caterpillars with a hatred which she could not overcome. The sight of them made her feel sick, as the sight of a cat does some otherwise quite ordinary people. She had lived in towns all her life, and had never approached the creatures near enough to see their points of interest. She just stood at a distance and shuddered.

Francesca was in very high spirits that day. She could not imagine that any one could be really afraid of a harmless stag-beetle, and thought that Monica's attitude was simply silly. She jigged up and down on one leg, waving the beetle gently in the air. 'Cowardy—cowardy-custard!' she chanted. 'Towny people are all cowardies. 'Fraid of cows—and dogs—and rats—and rabbits—and *all* the jolly things!'

'I'm *not* afraid of *any* of those!' Monica retorted, stung.

'Oh yes, you are! You *know* you are!' A demon had entered into Francesca and she flung her taunts without a thought. 'You're afraid of cows; you *said* you were!'

'I went through the middle of herds of them at Cambridge!'

'Only with me and the boys there to protect you! You're afraid of rats, anyway!'

'I'm not. There's an archway at home, and they run under it in the night. It's on my way home.'

'An' I bet you never go under it in the dark! I bet you wouldn't sleep on the hay-stack all one night! There!'

'I would,' Monica said loftily, 'if there was any sense in it!'

'Hoo! That's an easy way out! You wouldn't.' Then she relented. 'I'm going to take this thing in and put him in a box,' she said. 'Come too.'

'I won't. I hate him. Robin, I *wish* you'd put him down.'

'I won't. I want him.' With that she disappeared, and Monica was left to sulk.

She avoided Francesca for the rest of the morning, and hardly spoke to anybody. She found everything very dull. After lunch she wandered into the garden again. Just ahead of her she spied Mildred walking with the games-mistress. She would go and talk to them. They had both been very nice to her ever since she had won the Junior Championship. She hurried her steps and walked beside them. Mildred turned to her with a little vague smile. 'Hullo, kid! What do you want?' she said.

'Oh, nothing. Just some one to talk to.'

'Where's Robin?'

'Don' know!'

The games-mistress turned to her too, and said a word or two. But a frown had settled on Mildred's face and she maintained a glum silence. The games-mistress was young and rather shy, and her companion's gloom very soon froze her, so that the three were presently pacing along in a silence that simply bristled with discontent. Soon Monica could bear it no longer, and detached herself from them without a word. They passed her a short time afterwards, and Mildred was all smiles and talk again, and the games-mistress was laughing.

'They don't like me really, even yet,' she told herself miserably. 'They just put up with me, because I'm clever, and can play tennis, and because they like Robin. Oh, I hate them, I hate them! Now I haven't got Robin, and they won't even tolerate me!' She was stumbling indoors. But at that minute Robin came out, and linked her arm absently, as usual, in her friend's. 'Couldn't find you anywhere,' she said. 'Where were you?'

Monica broke into dimples. She never could resist Francesca's friendliness. 'Sulking,' she said.

'Oh, *Monnie*! You old gump! 'Cause I laughed at you?'

Monica nodded.

'Sorry,' Francesca said simply. 'I didn't mean to be horrid. Only—they're such harmless things! They can't even pinch. Never mind that, though. Where were you sulking?'

Monica's face grew bleak again. 'I tried to talk to Mildred and Miss Yates,' she said. 'But they simply wouldn't have me. Why don't they like me, Robin?'

Robin stood still and stared at her. 'D'you mean—you tagged on to them? Just those two?'

'Yes. Why not?'

Francesca chuckled. Somehow she always knew everybody's business in the House, just by looking on at them. 'You old silly—Mildred's most *terrifically* keen on Miss Yates! She'd simply want to *kill* you if you butted in when she'd got her to herself!'

Monica looked bleaker than ever. 'I didn't know,' she said. 'How *could* I know?'

'Well,' said Francesca wisely, 'when you see a mistress and a girl together, just walking about, obviously not on business, it's generally that. I don't like Miss Yates—she *lets* people be keen on her. Do you?'

'No. I don't know. I don't think about her. I shall *never* get on with them, Robin. I never know what they're thinking about.'

Francesca skipped, and shook Monica's arm. 'Oh yes, you will. Besides, you don't *want* to get on with Miss Yates specially, do you? And Mildred's—oh, just an old funny.'

'I don't *like* them to hate me,' Monica said. 'Then there's Mavis—' And she went on to the story of Mavis's sneer at her pyjamas.

'She has got 'em a bit over those pyjamas,' Francesca acknowledged. 'I heard her boasting about them the other day.

Any one 'ud think she'd never had any decent ones before, the fuss she makes about them. Ordinary people would just take them as a matter of course.'

Monica grinned slowly. 'I never thought of that,' she said. 'They're just a new toy! I say, you do know a lot!'

'Oh—bishy-bosh!' gurgled Francesca. 'I only watch people. It's fun.'

CHAPTER XIV.

AN ADVENTUROUS NIGHT.

THE black day dragged on to its dull end. Monica was out of humour with everything, even in spite of Francesca's refusal to behave as though they had quarrelled. She knew the girls all disliked her, she was certain of it; and certain, suddenly, that Francesca despised her for their dislike, underneath her apparent friendliness.

'Silly, she's liked you ever since you first met her,' Monica's more sensible half said.

'Not specially,' the disgruntled half objected. 'She's like that to every one.'

'She doesn't have every one to stay with her.'

'Oh—well, she was sorry for you. Anyway, she thinks you're a coward!'

Out of that brooding grew her wild plan. Francesca had said she was afraid of rats, that she wouldn't dare to spend a night on a haystack. She would just show her. She would spend that very night as ever was on the haystack in the school grounds. Robin should see what a mistake she had made.

She went off quietly to bed with every one else, and waited, wide-eyed, for the seniors and then the mistresses to go to their rooms too. It seemed ten times as long as usual before the house was quiet that night. When at last it was, she slipped out of bed and dressed herself. It would be cold, lying out there all night long. She put on a woolly coat under her faded dressing-gown, and folded a blanket off her bed to take with her. She arranged the pillow to make a hump in the bed, took her thick shoes in her hand, and crept downstairs.

She had thought it all out. The Junior room was the farthest room on the ground floor from the mistresses' quarters, and it had windows which opened outwards. She could climb out of one of them easily, and slink in the shadow of the wall until she came to the kitchen garden, and there the trees and plants would shelter her.

The Junior room was filled with moonlight. It looked very big and bare, and some of the corners were very dark. Resolutely she turned her back on them and fumbled with the window. It opened without a sound. She dropped her blanket out, put on her brogues and thrust her bedroom slippers into her pocket, and jumped after it. She found she could just reach to shut the window gently after her, then stole along on the grass to the garden gate.

There she paused, suddenly made oblivious of everything by the beauty of the night; above all, by its stillness and its faint, fresh smell, and the cool brush of the wind on her face. The moon was sailing high and dipping under the wisps of cloud. The waves were swishing softly on the shore in the distance, dragging the pebbles after them as they drew back baffled, gathering themselves together for each muffled thud. Monica had never been out late at night before. Nature seemed to be holding her breath. What could Monica do but tread softly and do the same?

She was bending to open the gate when suddenly something happened which brought her upright again. A fairy piping began in the trees in front of her—one tiny, questioning note, then a pause, and then another.

'It's a nightingale!' Monica whispered. She had never heard one before. She stood breathless, listening for more. It came—a few more trial notes, and then the full tripping, tumbling song. She stood till the bird had finished, then gave one look at the

House behind her. One of the darkened windows showed a lighter blot in the middle. Some one else attracted by the nightingale, Monica thought. Would she be able to hear him from the haystack, she wondered. If she could, she would not mind how many rats came, or how many nights she spent there.

She went on past the apple-trees and strawberry beds. As she opened the farther gate, a tentative 'Wuff!' made her jump. She had forgotten that the sheep-dog pup had his kennel there. She shut the gate quietly and went forward to him. 'Bob! Bob—it's me!'

The rigid, furry body became a wriggling, fawning mass as the dog recognised her voice, pawing to reach her face, slobbering over her shoes.

Suddenly she decided to take him with her. He would be company for her, and he would scare the rats too. She unhitched his chain, and he rolled at her feet, then sped away into the darkness. She heard him crashing among the plants. Silly, stupid of her to let him off. He would wake the gardener, and she would be caught, and there would be a rumpus. In a minute he was beside her again, and she took hold of his collar and told him fiercely to go to heel, which, luckily for her, he very meekly did.

She reached the haystack at last. There was a very convenient, cosy-looking ledge half-way up, sheltered from the wind but open to the moonlight. She almost purred as she looked at it. She thought she must have been a tramp once, before she was a schoolgirl, so inviting did it seem to her.

Then she heard a rustle in the hay, and another, and another. There *were* rats. She nearly turned and ran back to her bed. Bob leaped forward and buried his face in a hole and sniffed and snorted, and the rustling miraculously stopped. She was *very* glad she had brought Bob.

She found a little ladder and clambered up it; wriggled in under the hay, Bob beside her; spread the blanket over her and peeped over the top of it, eyes and ears alert.

Didn't people go mad if they slept in the moonlight? She didn't see why they should. It was probably all rubbish, she decided. All bishy-bosh, Francesca would have said. She wished Francesca could have been there with her. She would have enjoyed it. Perhaps they could do it again one night, both together. She wriggled farther into the hay. It was very nice and warm, and she loved the cool wind on her face. She was actually enjoying it.

What was that? A rustle again? Bob sat up and cocked an ear, and the sound ceased. Then came a queer little thudding on the ground below her. 'Rabbits!' she thought delightedly. 'Rabbits, drumming with their back-legs to talk to each other! I wonder if it really is!'

Heaps of other little noises there were, too; little squeakings and scufflings and twitterings. At first she sat up every time one came; but they never seemed to come near her, and gradually she grew used to them. Perhaps Bob kept them away. She felt quite safe with Bob. She was getting very sleepy.

When she woke up, there was a cold light all round her. The stars were scarcely visible in the pale blue sky. Away in the east, a golden caterpillar crawled along the edge of a dull gray bank of cloud just showing above the downs. A cock crowed, a flock of sparrows awoke and squabbled, ducks quacked and walked across the farmyard in a long, single file; all the birds tried their voices.

Monica looked at her watch. Five o'clock. Actually she did not want to go in. She need not, just yet. She was quite warm, and felt fresh and lively. Bob was sleeping quietly beside her. She waited until the sun sprang up over the cloud-bank,

She found a little ladder and clambered up it.

scattering it and burning the golden caterpillar up in crimson smoke. Then she gathered up her blanket and slid down. She kept Bob beside her until she chained him to his kennel again. She went almost carelessly towards the house. She did not care much if somebody did see her. She had done it, and it was worth whatever happened to her. She reached the window safely and unhooked it, hurled her blanket in, pulled herself up by her hands and scrambled in too, and so, swiftly, to the dormitory and bed.

Her bed was very smooth, after the tickly hay. But it did not smell nearly so good, and the ceiling was a poor substitute for the blue sky and the fading stars. She curled up, and dreamed of rustling rats and thumping bunnies until the seven o'clock bell clanged.

* * * * * *

At breakfast, and between lessons for the first half of the morning, she let Francesca talk about the ordinary gossip of the House. She must have a long time to tell her all about the night, not sandwich the story between Latin and algebra.

At break she guided Francesca's steps gently towards the haystack. Francesca, chattering all the time, hardly noticed where they were going. Opposite her ledge, Monica stopped. 'I slept there last night,' she remarked carelessly, as Francesca paused.

Francesca pushed at a toadstool with her foot. '*I* sha'n't rise,' she said placidly. 'Try again.'

Monica was faintly annoyed. 'You said I wouldn't spend a night on a haystack,' she said. 'Well, I did. I spent *last* night on *this* haystack, on that ledge.'

Francesca stood back and surveyed her. 'Are you—aren't you—pulling my leg?' she asked doubtfully. 'Honest?'

'Of course I'm not pulling your silly stick of a leg!' Monica snapped. 'I tell you, I spent last night on this haystack. I—I *enjoyed* it! I didn't want to come in!'

'You *are* pulling my leg!' Francesca said decidedly.

Monica heaved a sigh and looked away. 'There was a nightingale.' She enumerated the items on her fingers. 'And rats. And rabbits. And this morning there was a cock, and some ducks, and some birds. And the sun came up over there, all red. Oh, Robin, it was *lovely*!'

'Monica! Tell me, truth and honour, did you *really* do it?'

'Really and truly and honestly, Robin.'

Francesca drew a long breath. 'I never meant you to,' she said penitently. 'Weren't you awfully frightened?'

'Not a bit. Not a little bit!' Monica boasted.

'Didn't you mind the rats?'

'No. They didn't come near me, they only ran about.'

'Wasn't it cold?'

'Rather not. Hay's awfully warm stuff. It was simply, simply lovely; an' I never want to sleep indoors any more—except when it rains, of course.'

'*Monica!* Really and truly?'

'Really and truly.'

Francesca thought it all over. 'I shouldn't have minded all the other things,' she said presently; 'but I don't think I could have stood the rats. I'm—I'm terrified of rats.'

'I didn't mind 'em,' Monica said indifferently.

'You're awfully brave,' Francesca admired. 'I say—I'm sorry I said townies were cowards. They aren't, not a bit.'

'I knew that, of course,' said Monica loftily. 'Only I had to convince you.'

'*Now*,' Francesca said, seizing her arm, 'tell me all about it, every little bit—where you got out and everything!'

So Monica sketched her progress from the time she crept

out of bed. But she said nothing at all about Bob. Francesca just listened, with little squeaks of delight. And Monica was happy; she was being admired again.

* * * * * *

It was at tea-time on that same day that Francesca came up to her with a puzzled face. 'I say,' she began, 'you haven't been telling any one else about last night, have you? There'll be an awful row if it gets known, you know.'

'Of course I know. No, I haven't told any one except you. Wouldn't be such an ass.'

'Well, *I* haven't told a single soul,' Francesca went on. 'You believe that, don't you?' she added anxiously.

''Course, if you say so. Besides, you wouldn't.'

Francesca smiled at that. 'I know. Well, look here, somebody's publishing rumours—just little silly rumours—that you were out in the grounds last night, talking to some one at the garden gate.'

Monica was suddenly panic-stricken. Now she would be expelled, and would never go to Cambridge, and never be famous at all. 'Who—who's saying that?' she asked.

'I think it's Mavis.'

Then Monica remembered the white blot at the window which she had seen when the nightingale stopped singing. The window had been on her own floor, in her own dormitory; Mavis's window.

She told Francesca about it, and Francesca whistled. 'She saw you, did she! I say, that's bad.'

'What will she do?' Monica whispered. 'What will she do, Robin?'

Francesca was thinking hard, her brows knit. 'If I were she,' she said, 'I should try to find out more about it before I told people. I should *think* she'd do that. She's awfully curious.'

'Yes? What else?'

'I should think she'd watch for a night or two, to see if you do it again,' Francesca said.

'And when she finds I don't?'

'Tell the other prefects, or the mistresses, in a rage.'

'Then they'd ask me,' Monica went on, plucking miserably at her tunic; 'and—and I'm *rotten* at telling lies!'

Francesca was thinking deeply. 'Monnie,' she burst out presently, 'have you ever walked in your sleep?'

'Yes—no—I don't know. I believe I used to when I was little.'

'Sure?'

'Yes, I think so. Mother said so once.'

'Then *that* won't be a lie, and your people'll back you up if they're written to.'

'What *do* you mean?' Monica asked, astonished.

'Don't you see, you silly? You must walk in your sleep to-night! Go past Mavis's door so that she hears you, and she'll follow you. Then you can lead her round the passages a bit, looking all blank and asleep, you know—look at her and pretend you don't see her, and answer questions if she asks, because they always do—and then go back to bed. She'll feel an awful idiot, specially if she's told lots of people.'

Monica dimpled, relief in her eyes. 'Robin—you're just a genius!'

'D'you think you can do it?'

'Yes. Shall I try now?'

So they retired to a passage, and Monica swayed along with her eyes fixed and her hands stretched before her; and were nearly caught by a hurrying prefect, so uncontrollable did Francesca's giggles become.

CHAPTER XV.

MUD AND VANITY.

THAT night, Monica again lay awake until the House was quiet. She did not wait as long as the night before. She did not want Mavis to have dropped asleep, should she be carrying out Francesca's conjecture and watching.

She did not dress this time. It was very warm, and she was not going to sleep out of doors. She stole along the corridor, her hands stretched in front of her, her eyes peering eagerly round. Yes, Mavis's door was ajar. She shuffled with her feet, so that Mavis should not miss her; and Mavis's head appeared, very very quietly, round the door's edge.

Monica sped on, down the stairs, her heart jumping with excitement, chuckles rising in her throat. She turned the corner at the bottom, and then waited, as if she were thinking, her face turned towards the way she had come, her eyes a-stare. Mavis, turning the corner as she followed, pulled up with a start, and drew back. Monica glared full at her, through her, at the wall behind her, never moving a muscle of her face.

'Why,' she heard Mavis whisper, 'she's asleep!' The disgust in her tone tickled Monica so intensely that she had to turn away hastily so as not to laugh in Mavis's face. As she did so, a wicked idea came into her head. Mavis was resplendent in her silk pyjamas and satin dressing-gown and shoes.

Monica glided along the passage to the Junior room, flung open the door, and made straight for her window, undid its catch and vaulted out. She heard a gasp from Mavis behind her, and then, to her delight, the thud of Mavis alighting on the grass. The idea was going to come off!

She set off for the kitchen-garden, Mavis hard on her heels. The grass was drenched with dew, and she kept resolutely on it. She hardly noticed the damp through her thick felt slippers, and her shrunken pyjama-legs were well up out of the way. She held up her dressing-gown in her hands.

In the kitchen-garden she went straight across the lumpy, loamy beds instead of round the path. Mavis would tell everybody what had happened, so foot-marks did not matter. She went through a hole in the hedge into the farm-yard. It was dirty, that farm-yard, muddy and well caked with manure. Her short-cut lay across the manure-heap itself. She took it unhesitating, hoping with all her might that Mavis would not go round. And Mavis, intent on her pursuit, did not. Monica was making for the pig-styes. At the end of the row of them she stopped, and peered into the first. 'Monica!' she heard Mavis pant beside her, 'where are you going?'

Monica raised her head and stared through her pursuer again. 'The eggs!' she said. 'The eggs I laid here last night! They're here. I must find them. They want—they want some bread and butter.'

Mavis gasped. And Monica nearly laughed again at her own gibberish.

There were pigs in the first sty, and in the second. The third was empty, but ankle-deep in mud. Monica unlatched the little gate and crept in; and could almost have hugged Mavis when Mavis followed her.

She looked up, beaming. 'Ten!' she said clearly. 'Ten little nigger boys. All safe.'

She came out again then, latching the gate carefully behind her; and chortled inside herself when she realised that Mavis could not reach the catch from inside and was having to climb over. The gate was tarry.

Her progress back again was swift and direct. She climbed in at the window, Mavis panting behind her. Then, in the Junior room, flooded with moonlight, she stopped and swayed uncertainly, rubbed her eyes, and looked wildly round her. 'What am I doing? Where am I?' she cried. Then she seemed for the first time to see Mavis. 'Why have you brought me here?' she demanded. 'Why are you all muddy? Why, I'm muddy too!'

Mavis tried to take hold of her hand, but she hit out savagely. 'Leave me alone!' she said. 'What are you doing to me?'

'Come to bed,' Mavis said in a queer, stifled voice. 'Come, quick, you'll get cold.'

'I'm not cold, I'm hot,' Monica retorted querulously. 'How can I go to bed like this?' she argued, at the top of her voice, all the way up the stairs, with the desired result that the house-mistress pounced out of her bedroom and asked them what in this earth they were doing, awake and plastered with mud, at that time of night. 'Where *have* you been? You smell simply awful!' she added.

'I don't know—I don't know,' Monica moaned, and burst into tears of excitement.

Miss Mason put a comforting arm round her, and they both listened to Mavis's fluent story of the expedition. Miss Mason did not seem to entertain a single doubt of the truth of her explanation.

'I knew she was asleep,' Mavis said, 'because she looked right through me as though I wasn't there, and talked nonsense about eggs. I followed her because I thought she might hurt herself.'

'Quite right; very creditable,' Miss Mason murmured, and Monica's eyes twinkled behind their dropped lids. That was all right. She did not want to get Mavis into a row, the devastation of her clothes was revenge enough.

'Have you walked in your sleep before, Monica?' the house-mistress asked.

'I've heard mother say I used to,' she answered innocently. 'I don't remember it, of course.'

'Last night—last night,' Mavis burst in. 'I saw her!'

'Last night too! Dear me. Well, you'd better both come and be dried. I'm afraid your beautiful dressing-gown and slippers won't be fit for much again, Mavis; not in the decorative line, anyway. The pyjamas we can deal with, I expect.'

The matron was called, and the two explorers were dried, and warmed with hot drinks. Monica sat and hugged herself in front of the gas-fire. Had ever any plan answered so splendidly? Her own reputation was out of danger, and Mavis's spiteful sneers had been amply avenged. The satin slippers were two little wads of muddy rag; the dressing-gown was drenched and mud-stained nearly up to its waist, and had tar-marks on it. These could never regain their proud beauty. The pyjamas were muddy too, but they could be washed. Mavis had looked a sorry figure when she had trailed upstairs from the Junior room.

Monica's dressing-gown was also dirty, of course, but it had been washed so often before that another scrubbing could make not the slightest difference to it.

And so, their cocoa finished and clean clothes on them, Monica went triumphant, and Mavis chastened, to bed.

* * * * * *

'Monica! You're just a genius!' Francesca breathed when she heard the story the next day.

'It was your idea,' Monica modestly disclaimed.

'Only the tiniest bit of it. I only meant you just to swizzle her about the sleep-walking. But to squash her horrid conceit, and yet keep her out of Miss Mason's bad books, was just gorgeous!'

'Well, I couldn't've got her into a row, could I? It wouldn't have been fair.'

''Course it wouldn't. But it was a good thing you thought of it. Why were you so keen to have Mas out to see you? You could easily have gone back to bed without any one knowing.'

Monica laughed. 'Well, for one thing, I didn't want to go to bed all wet and dirty,' she said; 'and matron had got my clean pyjams. And for another, I thought Mavis might as well declare publicly what she had found me doing, so that there shouldn't be any doubt that she did declare it.'

Francesca nodded appreciatively. 'Yes, you've a brain,' she allowed. And Monica chased her joyously.

* * * * * *

But later in the morning, Monica doubted whether she had really been as clever as she had imagined. The portress came to the Lower Fifth room and said something to the mistress who was taking the class.

'Will Monica Baxter please go to Miss Mason at once?' the mistress announced.

Monica's heart went down to her boots. Had some one else seen her, and was the whole fraud found out? She slipped out of the room, her face burning under the gaze of the form, her spirits raised only for a second by Francesca's encouraging wink.

An unknown lady stood by the fire in the house-mistress's room.

'This is Doctor Adams, Monica,' Miss Mason said cheerfully. 'She's just going to have a look at you after your escapade last night.'

Monica answered the doctor's questions absently, her mind racing along all the possibilities. Would this woman say she wasn't to work so hard, and make her lie down instead of going to Latin or geometry or something, as one of the girls had to who had a weak heart? Or would she say she wasn't to play games, and make her give up the championship to Mildred?

The doctor looked at her tongue and felt her pulse and listened to her heart. 'She's sound enough, of course,' she said. 'Looks splendid.—Working too hard, old lady?'

'Not a bit,' Monica maintained stoutly. 'I don't do any more than any one else.'

'Playing too hard, then? Just won a championship, haven't you?'

'Perhaps—' Miss Mason was beginning, when Monica cast caution to the winds and stopped her. She had better make a clean breast of it all. They would punish her, of course; but they mustn't, they simply must not treat her as an invalid and cut off her work and her tennis.

'It wasn't that!' she burst out. 'It wasn't that at all, Miss Mason, please!'

The doctor smiled at her patiently. 'Something on your mind, had you?' she said.

'Yes. At least—you see, Francesca said I was a coward because I wouldn't play with her stag-beetle. I hate stag-beetles. She said I was afraid of rats and rabbits, and lots of other things that I don't mind a bit. And then she said I wouldn't dare to spend a night on a haystack—'

The doctor pounced like a swallow on a gnat. 'Splendid! Splendid! Why, you made like an arrow for the farmyard, didn't you? The haystack's in the farmyard, of course. Tell me,' she turned to Monica with an encouraging look; 'you were worried, I suppose, because your friend called you a coward?'

'I was angry,' Monica told her. 'I'm not a coward, really. I just don't like insects. I wanted to show her I wasn't.'

'That's right. That's right. And in sleep your subconscious self takes command, and leads you straight to the place you've marked in your mind by day as the place you'll show her in. That's very interesting; very interesting indeed.'

Monica was struck dumb by these learned explanations.

'Does your friend still think you're a coward?' the doctor inquired. 'Is it still worrying you?'

'Not—not very much,' said Monica at random.

'Don't let it worry you. I'll talk to your friend for you,' the doctor said kindly. 'I don't think we shall need to treat you any more. No medicines, or early bed, or anything—'

Monica heaved a breath of relief. This funny little lady had taken matters completely into her own hands. It was not going to be necessary to confess after all.

'We can simply remove the cause. That'll be all right, child. Don't you worry any more.—I should like to see the friend—Francesca, didn't you say?—if I may, Miss Mason.'

Miss Mason looked a little dubious. Perhaps she guessed more about the incident than she ever admitted.

'Send Francesca along, will you, Monica?' she said. 'You can go.'

Monica escaped, her mind full of a terrible problem: How was she to let Francesca know that Miss Mason and the doctor did not yet know the true history of the two nights? Francesca was still in her place in the French class, and that class would not be over for half-an-hour. There was nothing she could do. She would just have to trust to Francesca's wits; after all, they were the best wits.

She gave the message calmly to the French mistress, and watched Francesca's comically astonished face as it was repeated to her. She turned on that face a horrible grimace and an anguished wink as it went out of sight, and Francesca nodded, solemnly, ever so slightly.

The rest of that lesson was torment. Then Francesca came back, looking as innocent as a woolly lamb. As soon as the mistress had gone, Monica sprang on her. 'What happened?'

Francesca pursed her lips primly. 'You're not to be teased, not at all,' she told Monica. 'Dr Adams says so. You're not a coward; you're the bravest little girl—she said "little girl"—that ever was. Only you've got a "phobia"—good word—for stag-beetles, that you can't control. And my cruel words the other day preyed on your infant mind and made you try, even in your sleep—because there hadn't been time before you went to bed—to show me how brave you were. An' I'm to take back those words. Dar—ling Monica, I never meant them! Forgive me, can you? Can you ever forgive me?' All this with the gravest face one can imagine; then they caught each other's eyes and burst into peals of laughter.

'Oh, lovely! Rich and rare!' Francesca chortled. 'I thought you must've confessed when they started talking about haystacks. Then they got back to walking in your sleep and having things on your mind—and I knew you hadn't.'

'I jolly nearly did,' Monica said soberly; 'only the doctor headed me off. I like that doctor.'

Francesca nodded. 'And you score, all along the line,' she said.

CHAPTER XVI.

FOR THE HOUSE.

WHETHER or no Miss Mason had any suspicions as to the truth of Dr Adams's explanation of Monica's night out, it is certain that Evelyn, the head of Mason's, and her two friends, Erica and Penelope, brought shrewd eyes and wily brains to bear on the matter. They, too, had suffered from Mavis's pride in her new clothes. Her conversation had been almost entirely about them since the term started. And they were beginning to think that Monica was not so entirely ignorant of human nature as she had appeared to be during the previous term. That Francesca was by no means ignorant of it they had not a doubt.

To whatever conclusion they came, when Miss Mason told Evelyn sadly that she would have to transfer one of her prefects to the School House at once, because one School House prefect had suddenly left and another gone sick, they were unanimous as to who that prefect should be.

'I think Mavis Staddon had better go,' Evelyn told the house-mistress when they had talked it over. 'She's very keen, and quite a good prefect in her way. But she doesn't get on too well with our juniors. I don't think we squash them quite enough for her.'

'I had thought of her too,' Miss Mason agreed. 'Send her along as you go back, will you, and I'll tell her. D'you think the juniors are too rowdy, Evelyn?'

'Oh no. They're obedient enough. They rile Mavis a bit with their jibes. She's got no sense of humour at all. I think she'd like the School House better; they're much more solemn.'

The house-mistress smiled. 'We'd rather have them—not so solemn, I think. Don't you?' she said.

'*I* would. I'm glad you would too.'

'They turn out better, I think. One can't be solemn and keen about trivialities all one's life, and the sooner one learns to see big the better. Right, I'll see Mavis now.'

* * * * * *

Generally when a girl is transferred from one House to another at Greystones, there are terrible wailings and moanings; heart-searchings as to the reason for the change; heart-burnings as to which House, the old or the adopted, is *really* the better of the two. But in Mavis's case there was no question about any of these things. She took for granted that she was chosen to go to the School House because she was the steadiest and best of Mason's Sixth-formers; she chattered about her many friends in the School House and the few in Mason's who were worthy of her affection; and lauded up the School House until every one was sick of its very name, and vowed that it should be beaten in games and work and general behaviour and everything else.

So Sausage-face disappeared from Mason's. And it seemed to Monica that there was now nothing at all in the way of her steady climb to success. Success and popularity were what she craved, though she confessed it to no one except Francesca.

'Success—yes. That's sense. We said we'd be famous, and if you're famous you leave—oh, you leave things better than you found 'em. Raise the standard, leave a bit of knowledge behind you. But popularity doesn't matter a straw. All the grandest people have been unpopular till they've been dead.'

'Not much good being popular when you're dead,' Monica grumbled.

'Silly, there is. Gives people something decent to think about—Nelson, and Nurse Cavell, and people like that. That's how *I'd* like to be popular; not have people flocking round and saying how *charming* I was!'

'Oo—om! P'r'aps,' Monica doubtfully agreed. 'I wish people did like me more, though.'

'They will, when you get less frightened of them,' Francesca prophesied wisely. 'You're much better than you were, aren't you?'

And Monica laughed and allowed that she was.

* * * * * *

The preoccupation of the hour was now centred in the School Tennis Championships. The five Houses played against each other, juniors against juniors, and seniors against seniors. Monica and Francesca practised religiously whenever they had a minute to spare. It was rumoured that they were easily the best of the five pairs of juniors, but, it being a convention that House champions did not play against each other until after the ties were over, they had no means of knowing; and they were taking no risks.

The saga of their successes in that tournament would fill a book, should it ever be sung. They drew Pearson's, the holders and favourites, in the first round, and Mason's second seniors played theirs and lost badly; Francesca and Monica, stern and cautious at first, unable to resist their high spirits later, placing absurdly and racing about, won easily, and drew the two Houses level; and Mason's first couple, Erica and Evelyn, won their tie with a meagre margin and the match for Mason's.

Then there was a pause for Mason's, while the losers of that round played each other. Pearson's won, of course, and Mason's went on to their match against Richardson's, the other winners, and beat them easily, winning every game. Then Pearson's played the School House, and surprisingly lost; so that Mason's and the School House met in the final.

Excitement ran high, and the chances of the rival Houses were the only topic talked of at meals. The School House had beaten Pearson's by more than Mason's had, and so some people were sure it would beat Mason's; others said that the win from Pearson's was a fluke. One of the School House second couple sprained her wrist two days before the match was to be played—would she be better? Who would play instead? Would Mavis Staddon play, or would her feeling for her late House prevent her? Mavis herself soon put that notion to rout, and was to be seen practising assiduously with the surviving member of the pair.

She appeared on the day itself in the champion's white; and poor Dorothy, the real player, nursed her wrist and looked on.

The second couple always played first in these matches, perhaps because the juniors might be expected to be nervous if they had the striking of the first ball, and the firsts were required for the winning stroke. In any case Francesca and Monica watched, with unmoved faces but every feeling of bliss, the beating of Mavis and her partner by the two Upper Fifth-formers who were Mason's second pair. Mavis's tennis was as solemn as her other performances. She played very steadily, but seemed to follow a fixed routine and never rose to an opportunity; so that Mason's, true to the traditions of the House by being much more erratic and original, often won a game after an apparently forlorn hope. The tie ended eight-seven in favour of Mason's.

Monica and Francesca went into the pavilion to take off their coats and put on their rubber shoes. When they came out again they found one of the School House juniors waiting for them. The other was nowhere to be seen.

'Where's Connie?' they asked.

Nobody appeared to know.

'Go and find her, some one. Anywhere you can think of,'

the games-mistress commanded; and a legion of juniors trotted away in various directions.

They waited ten minutes. Then one of the searchers came back with the news that Connie was doing a music exam., and that the examiner had been late, and she would not be finished for another quarter of an hour.

'She ought to have had it at two,' the junior explained, 'but he didn't come till after three.'

'Poor Connie! Go and tell her we'll wait for her,' said Miss Yates. 'And we'll play the first couples now and the juniors after tea.'

It was the only thing to do. But it seemed to Mason's that the change of plan had changed their luck; for Erica and Evelyn, that redoubtable couple who had not yet been beaten, fell to the dull, steady, lobbing School House pair to the tune of six games to nine.

They came off the court with rueful smiles. 'Sorry, everybody! Simply couldn't do a thing against those lobs! It's the deadliest game to play.' Which the School House had very probably known when they sized up their swift, dashing opponents.

Monica and Francesca were wild with excitement. The games now were sixteen to the School House and only fourteen to Mason's. They, the junior couple, had got to win by nine games to six to win the match. Could they possibly do it?

'Had we better lob, too?' Monica asked doubtfully. 'Wouldn't it be safer?'

Francesca shook a decided head. 'I don't think so. I think we've got to be just as wild an' woolly as we can, to put them off, so that they simply don't know what we're goin' to do next. Be careful, too, of course, but be wild an' woolly at first, even if it loses us a game, and then settle down and be cautious afterwards when they're not expecting it.'

'That's sense,' Monica approved.

Mason's won the toss, and Monica opened proceedings very differently from the usual beginning of a junior match game. She had got to frighten them; and she set her teeth and did it. She whizzed down two services in the very outermost corners of the courts; and the spectators laughed and clapped, and were angrily hushed by Mason's supporters lest they should disturb the players. The faces of the School House juniors grew long, and they retired to the back-line. So Monica served more gently, into the middle of the court; and her opponent raced forward in a hurry and returned straight into the net. The other junior did not know what to expect, and came tentatively forward to a midway position; whereupon Monica sent her a shot with a twirl on it that curved away sideways—and Mason's had won a love-game.

Francesca grinned as she walked back from the net. 'That's the stuff,' she said.

They found the gentle, steady School House service dull, but fairly easy to deal with. There were no wits behind it, or, if there were, they were not trained in the ways of tennis. Monica kept to the back-line and returned long, low pushes; and Francesca jigged and jumped at the net and killed anything that came her way, until that game was won too.

Francesca, with a wicked eye for effect on her enemy's moral, put on a face of lamb-like imbecility and served into the net, and then, very gently and childishly, into the middle of the court. The junior against her smiled with relief. This was better. She banged down a return across the court where it could not possibly be reached. Erica looked worried. Had Francesca lost her nerve? But Monica caught her friend's eye as they crossed over, and giggled.

Francesca served another silly serve, which was treated in

much the same way as the first—Monica hadn't a chance with it. Then she licked her lips in a way that meant business, and for the rest of the game the balls that left her racquet looked exactly as if they were going into the net, but somehow gave a miraculous little jump as they reached it, and hurtled over into the place where the striker was not. The School House juniors did not know where to arrange themselves. They advanced and retreated in little hops and jumps, and thought they were lucky if they managed to hit the ball at all.

In the next game, both Francesca and Monica aimed all their shots between the other two. Three times their rivals rushed together to the ball and stopped before either of them had hit it; and once they frankly collided and fell over each other.

'That's all right,' Francesca beamed. 'We've got 'em dithering now. Now we'll play proper tennis.'

And they proceeded to give such an exhibition of junior tennis as had never been seen at Greystones before. They hit hard (for Francesca's wiry arms had nearly as much strength in them as Monica's big ones) and used their brains. That was the gist of the matter. They knew each other's play so well that wherever one was not the other assuredly was when she was needed. They were not afraid to volley, and killed many good strokes by that deadly method. And they seemed to possess an uncanny instinct that told them where their opponents would put the ball. They lost points, of course. The School House pair were very good, in an ordinary game. But this was no ordinary game, and they were outclassed and bewildered. Rally after rally they played, deuce after deuce was scored. Once Monica missed an easy-looking return and lost a game to them. She nearly lost her temper then, but remembered in time the old episode on the hockey field, and that the House's performance in more than tennis was being watched by the crowd round the court. In the end Mason's won by twelve games to three—enough and to spare—the set, and the match, and the cup.

Crowds of Masonians pursued the junior couple into the House. Erica and Evelyn patted their backs, the games-mistress prophesied Wimbledon and international fame for them; and, but for Francesca's absurd, cynical gibes, their heads would have been completely turned. But Francesca was too sensible to be spoiled, and Monica was learning to see little matters like failure and success in sport through her friend's impartial eyes.

CHAPTER XVII.

AN ESCAPADE AND A CONFESSION.

THERE was pandemonium in Mason's that evening. There was allowed to be, after the House Cup had been won. The team and every one else who could crowd in ate an enormous and sugary tea. They all picked meagrely at supper; and later feasted in Erica's dormitory off ice-cream made in a pail by Penelope, and all sorts of decoctions sent from all sorts of people's homes, and queer drinks that fizzed and sparkled when they were stirred. The team was toasted and teased, and made to burst into speeches. Every one who possibly could was urged to entertain the rest. Francesca dashed off lightning sketches of every one who had a feature to her face; Monica danced and won great applause. Erica walked the length of the room on her hands; and all sorts of other pranks were played. The proceedings were wound up with an enormous pillow-fight, which went on until the mistresses, who had been discreetly immured in their common room, were heard to open and shut the door several times to indicate that they were coming to bed.

'Ten minutes grace they give us after this,' Erica told the breathless mob who assembled at her call. 'Well, it's been a good evening. We've won in all the games. Now, Evelyn here would say, we've jolly well got to win at bookwork as well. Not a fad; common-sense. She's goin' to get a schol., herself, for a start. And we want to have Masonians at the head of every form—for the House, not for themselves. See? Back to bed, now, every one.'

Monica prodded Francesca with her elbow, as one who

would say, 'I told you so.' And Francesca nodded absently and continued to look out of the window, across to the School House, where something had caught her eye while Erica had been speaking.

She caught Monica's hand as she was joining the crowd who straggled back to their own dormitories. 'Look,' she said; 'their flag's flying.'

Monica followed her pointing finger. 'Yes. Why not?'

'Conquered people,' said Francesca grandly, 'ought not to fly flags.'

Monica looked at her with big, mild eyes. 'No,' she agreed, 'they ought not.'

Francesca's brain was working furiously. She was mad with excitement to-night. 'Can't we take it down?' she asked.

'Take it down? Now?'

'Yes—when the mistresses have gone to bed.'

Monica chuckled, and the big eyes took a wicked look. 'It 'ud be awful fun!' she said. 'Can we get up there?'

'Yes.' Francesca sketched the plan which she had just evolved. 'Out of the Junior room. Into the School House through the pavilion; it's open this weather to keep the House cool. Then just up the spiral staircase to the roof, and it's done.'

'I bet we get caught,' Monica prophesied.

'But if we do, we can say you're sleep-walking again. It's a great idea, that sleep-walking.'

Monica looked doubtful. 'Ye—es, I s'pose we could,' she said. But she knew she would not escape from Miss Mason and the doctor a second time.

'Bed, you two!' Erica's voice came back to them and sent them scuttling.

'I'll come and fetch you when it's quiet!' Monica whispered as they went.

And so for a third night Monica slipped out of bed and crept, very cautiously this time, along the passage. Francesca joined her, and they went on, past the bathrooms. Francesca paused there. 'I say,' she whispered, 'don't you think Mavis is—a sort of Jonah to the School House? They *ought* to have won, you know.'

Monica grinned. It was just like Robin to discuss unimportant things like that at such a time and place.

'Don't you think,' Francesca went on, 'that we might show how we—disapprove of her?'

'How can we do that?' Monica whispered back.

Francesca looked mysteriously towards the linen cupboard, then cautiously opened its door and went in. She came out again with a seraphic smile—and a pair of pyjama trousers. 'I brought some scissors,' she murmured, 'in case we wanted to cut the rope. We'll cut the mark off. I don't know whose they are; there are heaps like 'em, so nobody'll know.' Which she neatly and speedily did, sitting on the edge of the bath.

'What *are* you goin' to do?' Monica asked her.

'Fly these!' Francesca gurgled.

They climbed safely out and safely reached the pavilion. Then they suffered a set-back, for the door from the pavilion to the House was locked. Francesca saved the situation by wriggling her small self through the hole cut in the door for the Head's cats to walk in and out, and let Monica in from the inside. To creep up the spiral staircase to the roof was easy. Then came a short squabble as to who was to walk along the wide parapet, visible in the moonlight to any one who should look, and actually do the deed. Finally they decided that Monica should do it because she was stronger, and Francesca should follow with the new 'flag.'

The House flag came down with a run, and made such a

squeak as it came that the two cowered fearfully at the foot of the pole, sure that the whole school must have been awakened. But no window was thrown up, no sound at all heard, and presently they dared to go on with their task. They tied the string of the pyjamas to the flag-rope, and pinned them to the rope at each side as well with safety pins which Francesca unhooked from under her collar. 'I always keep them there,' she said. 'I pick 'em up in the bathroom sometimes.'

Then they stole back to bed, and to sleep. And in the morning came successive gusts of laughter from each group that happened to go to the window and catch sight of the pyjama-legs, as proudly inflated with the breeze as any country-woman's washing on a fine day.

Nobody ever knew officially who the offenders were, though several people in Mason's, and one at least in the School House, made good guesses. And, because the outrage was perpetrated on one of the few nights when ragging was received with a blind eye and a deaf ear, the authorities made no inquiries.

'Everything seems to be settling itself at once,' Francesca said contentedly at lunch-time to Monica. 'Mavis out of the way and made to look a silly ass, and the tennis cup won.'

Monica looked doubtful, and eyed her friend anxiously. 'There's a thing that isn't settled,' she burst out at length.

'What?' Francesca inquired. 'Exams., d'you mean? They'll be on us soon enough.'

'No; didn't mean that. I say—I had Bob with me that night.'

'Bob! What night? When you swizzled Mavis?'

'No; the haystack night.' Monica poked the floor with her toe and stole a shame-faced look at Francesca. 'That's why I wasn't frightened.'

Francesca was silent for a minute. 'That was jolly sensible

of you,' she said at last. 'Rats are—a little bit dangerous, you know. Remember the bishop?'

'I did remember him,' Monica said. 'That's why I took Bob. I didn't—I didn't *mean* to take him, though. I meant to go by myself, however dangerous they were. Then I ran into his kennel on the way, and thought of it.'

'It was jolly brave of you,' said Francesca, 'even to *mean* to go. It would've been awful if the rats had eaten you up. I felt—I felt an awful pig for making you risk your life like that. I'm *glad* you took Bob.'

Monica stared at her. 'Why don't you—why don't you say *I* was an awful pig for not telling you?' she demanded.

'I don't think you were. Why should you tell me? I dared you to spend a night on the haystack, and you did. I didn't even say "by yourself."'

'But I *boasted*!' poor Monica protested. 'I said I enjoyed it!'

'Well, so you did, didn't you?'

'Ye—es. But I shouldn't have, without Bob.'

'You don't know. You might have. What was it you said wasn't settled?'

'That, of course. I've meant to tell you ever since I did it, only I funked. I thought you'd chuck me.'

'Thought I'd chuck you for not telling me?'

'Yes. I was mean.'

'Oh, bishy-bosh!' said Francesca.

Monica looked out of the window, full of the tremendous relief which follows the doing of some dreaded thing. 'I think—that's jolly decent of you!' she mumbled.

Francesca seized her arm and galloped with her out into the garden.

CHAPTER XVIII.

THE PINNACLE.

AFTER that, Monica settled down into something like the state she had been in before the advent of Francesca—like it, but not the same, for she was lured out by Francesca and many other people who were beginning to know her to the tennis-courts; and she spent the evenings in the Junior room talking and reading, not working surreptitiously. She had found for herself a much better axiom than 'Stick to your work and don't dissipate;' her own maxim had become, in effect, 'Work hard, and play hard, and don't worry about anything else;' which she faithfully did, having arrived at the decision to do it only through tribulation. She was one of those lucky people who possess the power of concentration. Her brain was not so much deep—she was not such a good thinker as Francesca—as keen-edged while she worked; she took in and remembered everything that came under her eye. That was why, when she had done nothing but work, she had so quickly got stale; her brain had taken in more than any head could possibly hold. Now that she allowed herself some recreation she found she could work harder than ever. And work she did, all the term, but quietly and methodically, not feverishly as she had done at first. She was, by inheritance, an almost entirely materialistic person. She concentrated on the matter in hand, and did not wander along by-roads of possibility or dream of other things. She did not know how to dream; but she knew how to deal very well with things as they came along. That was why she and Francesca were such a powerful combination later on. Monica supplied the will and the strength and the material genius; Francesca dreamed, and wheedled *people*, and left *things* to her friend.

Now, the important play that mattered to the House being over, they applied themselves more fiercely to work. The House had become a sort of god for Monica—no religious born in a faith is so full of zeal as a convert, and in the same way Monica's zeal was greater than that of the girls who had grown from babyhood in the doctrine that school, team, house, or what-not matter more than self. She had played and won for the House; now she must work and win for it.

Girls and mistresses watched her and discussed her.

'She'll crash in the exams.,' the mistresses said. 'She didn't do particularly well last term. People never do succeed outstandingly at both work and games; 'tisn't possible.'

Only the games-mistress demurred. 'She's splendidly healthy, and she's kept herself fit,' she said. 'That goes for a lot. She can stand more, and do more, than most girls. That ought to have some sort of a result.'

'There's nothing the woman doesn't know!' her own form told one another in amazement.

Francesca was at her elbow, admiring, egging her on. 'You've got to be top of every single thing,' she urged. 'If you're not, I shall be, an' you won't like that; though it won't matter really, as I'm Mason's too.'

Monica just grinned and went on working. 'People *can* be good at work and games too,' she said. 'But I don't think they can be very good *persons*—just as persons—if they are. There's no time.'

'*I* do that side,' Francesca said. 'People like me all right. Least, they seem to. I like them, anyway. And if they like me they'll like you too. We'll make one good person between us.'

Monica laughed. 'We sha'n't be together all our days,' she said ruefully.

'P'r'aps,' said Francesca wisely, 'we shall've absorbed a little of each other by the time we have to stop being together; so that you'll be able to deal with people a bit, and I with things a bit. Dogs get like their masters. Why shouldn't friends get like each other?'

* * * * * *

Francesca was top of English and Latin, and Monica of every single other thing in the Lower Fifth. Francesca went home for the long summer holidays laden with addresses and promises of letters. Monica had only one address—Francesca's. But she was very pleased with her term all the same. Francesca had solved *her* problems for her. She thought that she had found her niche.

EPILOGUE.

TWO juniors strolled across the garden of Mason's House on the first day of term. One, bright-eyed and eager, was being shown round by the other, who, veiling a mighty importance under a show of unconcern, kept a wary eye on her young sister's doings as she pointed out places and people to her.

As they came towards the House, they saw a pair of older girls race through the conservatory and down the steps, then fall into a jog-trot as they made for the games field, talking in breathless gasps, and now and then breaking into contented chuckles. The smaller one did most of the talking. She was thin, with great twinkling eyes and a mop of yellow-red hair. The other was tall and broad and very straight, with a little round head over which black short hair was sleekly brushed. This, and her rosy cheeks and dark eyes, and wide, curly mouth, made a great contrast with her thin, fair friend.

'Who are those?' the new girl inquired.

Her sister followed them with solemn eyes as long as they could be seen. Then she drew a long breath. 'Did you see?' she said. 'They waved to us!'

'Yes; of course I saw. Who are they?'

'The big one's Monica. She's simply—wonderful.' The girl's voice was husky with reverence. 'She's games captain. There's nothing she can't play better than everybody else, and we've never had such good teams as we have now. It's all because she coaches them so well. She won't stand slackness, or swank, or—or anything! She tells you where your play's wrong, and gives you a week or two to make it better, reminding you all the time. And if you *don't* make it better, she says she's sorry you'll have to go back to the beginners' game for the present, but that you could be good if you'd only try. And then, of course, you do try. She's topping to new girls, too.'

'How ripping!' the new girl said, impressed.

'That's not all, though. She's head of the House, too. She had to be—there wasn't any one else who could touch her at work. And she's just got a scholarship to Cambridge—a really grand one, with every one in England an' Scotland an' Ireland against her, not just a school affair. So this is her last term. Francesca's going there too; she's got the School Scholarship. Monica wasn't allowed to have them both. I don't know what the school'll do without them. It'll be simply *beastly*, *I* think.'

'Who's Francesca?'

'The other one—the little one. Every one simply *loves* Francesca. I don't know why, quite. She's a topping person. She always talks to people—any one, whatever she's like; and somehow, all one's best bits come out and show when she's there. P'r'aps that's why she can never find anything nasty to say about any one. She isn't like a Sixth Former—she treats every one as if they were as good as she is. But every one respects her all the same, and she can make you do as she wants, whoever you are. She's good at games, too; not quite as good as Monica, but jolly good—in the first eleven, and a tennis champion. And she draws and paints just beautifully. They simply run Mason's, those two. They're the most wonderful people we've ever had. Every one says so.'

'And yet they waved to us!'

'Oh yes. That's just like them; they're not stuck up, not a bit.'

The new girl looked towards the gate through which the pair had vanished. 'I should like to be like that,' she said thoughtfully.

THE END.

TWO SHORT STORIES BY JOSEPHINE ELDER

The two short stories that follow originally appeared in one or more of the various annuals for girls published by Oxford University Press.

We have chosen these particular stories to accompany *The Scholarship Girl* because they both, in different ways, deal with a similar theme: the integration of a 'difficult' or unusual new girl into a school.

To match the style of *The Scholarship Girl*, in these two short stories we have amended two instances of 'everyone' to 'every one' and three instances of 'anyone' to 'any one'.

Clarissa Cridland and Sarah Woodall
2011

Guide Isabella

ISABELLA was unpopular. There was no doubt about it. It was all because she was "queer." Her name was ridiculous. An Isabella ought to be tall and slim and dark, dignified and aloof, and the name should be followed by some liquid-sounding, stately surname. Isabella Huggins was a little button of a girl—a round red button for a nose, flat blue buttons for eyes peering timidly and widely about her, a mouth that as often as not had fallen open to show white buttons of teeth, and wispy fair hair which, even in the year 1925, was dragged back from her face by an Alice-in-Wonderland comb. Then her clothes were funny. She came to school in a velvet dress of rich brown, embroidered with oranges and red berries, instead of the regulation navy blue tunic; she ran about in flat sandals, and had bare legs in summer, and she never wore a hat. She was clever, too, in unusual ways; she could gabble French and

Italian as well as she could English, and translate Latin quite moderately without having prepared it; she knew more than any of them about history, and could tell the story of any of Shakespeare's plays without a thought; and she was always scribbling—"just things people say," she explained when she was asked what the scrawled lines were all about—and said she never spent more than twenty minutes over the English essay which cost every one else at least an anxious hour, and she always came out top. And, when she first came to the High School, she had never played a game or been in a gymnasium in her life. How could a girl like that—a little, shabby, useless button of a girl—expect to be tolerated, much less popular, in a big school in which everybody's aim was to be exactly like everybody else, but perhaps a bit better at games?

The tragedy was that Isabella did expect it. She had an enormous imagination, and she had imagined herself the heroine of a hundred amazing scenes. She would play as a substitute in a second eleven match and shoot a winning goal, and be tried for the first and get her colours. She would be head of her form and rule it with a rod of iron. She would be the only gym "leader" in the Lower Fourth. She would—and this was the most cherished "pretend" of them all—walk round the garden at "elevens" arm-in-arm with Valerie Carpenter, and sit next to her at dinner, and go to tea with her every Saturday.

But she was always put at back or goal at hockey, where one had no chance of shooting, and she was never tried even for the third eleven; she was very moderate at gym, and Valerie, who was a Sixth Form prefect, never took the slightest notice of her at all.

There came a time when even Isabella's imagination was not equal to the task of pretending that she was enjoying herself at school. She faced the facts pluckily enough—none of her ambitions were being realized, and something must be done. She looked about her. Valerie was captain of the Guides; she would join the Guides.

The Guides were not thrilled. Nobody wanted Isabella in her patrol. Nobody looked forward to the job of training her. "She'll have to get some proper clothes," they said. Isabella brought pressure to bear upon her family and did so, and for two days in the week was almost happy, for in uniform she looked more or less like every one else, and Valerie knew that she existed and sometimes even spoke to her. She surprised them all by knuckling down to her Guide work and passing her Tenderfoot tests at a bound. The Guides became her craze. She gave them all her thoughts and most of her energy, and very soon, if she was not a shining light among them, she at least did them no discredit.

She was happier; but she was still queer. The girls still looked askance at her, laughed about her a little, and, when they had to talk to her, explained things loudly and carefully as if she were a foreigner. She longed for the time when she should prove to them that she was not extraordinary, that she could do ordinary things just as they could, that she was as useful as they were.

One day it seemed that her opportunity had come. The Guides had somehow to augment their funds, and the High School Company was to give some sort of an entertainment to help. Great discussions were held to decide what exactly should be done, and Isabella sat on the floor and held her breath as the others talked. Would it be something that she could help with? If they acted a play, she knew instinctively that she would have no chance at all. Her insignificant looks and her little quiet voice would not even fit her for a chorus part. And what else than a play could they possibly contemplate? Then her heart gave a bound of relief, for it seemed that several companies were to join in an enormous gym display in the school hall. She was not bad at gym—not brilliant, but still not bad. She would be able to join in. Perhaps, if she worked very hard, she might even manage to shine a little bit and make the audience say that the High School Company was the best of them all. She came out of her dream to hear more of the discussion. It seemed that her patrol and two others were to give a display on the rings. She loved the rings—she could swing as high as anybody, and she was so little and light that she could pull herself up and turn and somersault without any trouble at all. She went home and to bed that night hugging herself with joy.

The next day the Blackbirds—Isabella's patrol—met in the gymnasium to practise. Isabella tugged mats across the room, and then stood rigidly at attention. She wanted to jig up and down with excitement, but she didn't. She had got to be a credit to the Guides, and she stood quite still.

The patrol leader swung high and turned; the second followed her, then the others in quick succession; and then it was Isabella's turn. She marched jauntily, stiffly, out of her place, stood for a second, then threw her arms up to grip the rings. She could not reach them. The rest of the patrol were all taller than she was by a head. What a nuisance! Well, she could jump.

She did jump, grasped first with one hand, then with both, and hung awkwardly for a second. She could not reach the ground even with the tips of her toes to get a push off. She pulled with her arms and made the whole of her body undulate in a vain effort to swing; but it was no good, and she heard the line of girls chuckling as she hung wriggling.

She jumped down and made for the corner where the pole was kept that was used to alter the length of the ropes. "I'll let them down a bit," she said.

She heard the line of girls chuckling as she hung wriggling.

The gym mistress, who was superintending the display, stopped her.

"Never mind now. We'll go on to the next."

The leader swung and pulled herself up shoulder high this time, and the others followed. When Isabella's turn came, the mistress put a hand on her arm.

"You stand aside this time, Isabella," she said. "We're a bit late as it is."

Isabella was disappointed, but that was all. Next time she would have the pole all ready, and perhaps they would not be in such a hurry. After all, it was rather important to have the rings lowered specially so that one could perform.

The next practice was at four o'clock the following day. Isabella went through all the movements in her head. She knew exactly what to do; it didn't really matter that she had had to miss that rehearsal before, not a bit. She was going to be most awfully good at this one.

"Prep" was over at a quarter to four, and she went down to the cloakroom with every one else. She was stowing her books in her satchel when she heard her name.

"Isabella, here a minute!"

Her patrol leader was standing at the door. She went out.

"You needn't bother to come this afternoon," the leader told her. "We are not going to want you for the display."

Isabella looked at her stupidly.

"Not—want me?" she said.

"No. You're too small. It would spoil the look of it all to lower the rings in the middle every time, and we can't all have them too low. We're getting Joan up from the Brownies to take your place." Then the look of hopeless despair on Isabella's face penetrated her well-meaning brain. "Bad luck," she said kindly. "P'r'aps we'll be able to find something else for you to do."

But Isabella shook her head. They didn't want her. She knew.

"There isn't anything," she said. "Thank you."

• • • • • • •

All the evening her thoughts whirled. She was too small. That was the excuse. If only she could grow, the excuse would be gone. One *could* grow. One could do anything by—by suggestion—her mother had said, if only one wanted it enough. You simply had to want hard all the time, and the thing came. She wished there was something else she could do as well as wanting. Just wanting was very nerve-racking. Perhaps—perhaps— She had an idea. She would wish all night, and if she hadn't grown enough by the morning—well, she would see.

In the morning her dress was not any shorter than usual. She went off to school with her face set—as determined as a round button of a face could be.

• • • • • • •

It was Valerie who found her. Valerie happened to walk through the gymnasium in the hour after lunch, when every one ought to have been in the garden. Valerie, being a Sixth Form prefect, was allowed to do what she liked with her free time, and she was on her way to the lab. to look at an experiment she had there.

She heard a funny little noise as she opened the door, and peered round to see where it came from. It had sounded rather like a stifled sob. She could see nothing, and she was just going out at the other end of the room when she heard it again. It came from a dark corner under the gallery, where a horizontal ladder ran along about six feet above the ground. Some one was hanging by her hands from that ladder.

As Valerie crossed the room, the person dropped in a heap

to the floor, and crouched there, biting her lips and whimpering and rubbing her shoulders.

"Isabella!"—Valerie stood over her in astonishment—"what on earth's the matter? What are you doing here? Why, you weren't at dinner, were you?"

Isabella struggled into a sitting position.

"I was here," she said. Then hastily, "I'm not crying, Valerie."

Valerie still looked puzzled.

"But what were you doing here?" she asked.

Isabella seemed to consider. Should she tell Valerie or not? Valerie would think her awfully silly. But then she probably did that already.

"I was trying to make myself grow," she said.

"I was trying to make myself grow," she said. "I thought if I stayed here a long time and—and stretched myself, I might. But it hurt so after a bit that I fell off."

Valerie looked at her with some interest. What a funny little thing she was! She must have wanted very badly to grow, to do a thing like that and go without her dinner and risk a row for being where she had no business to be.

"What did you do it for?" she inquired.

Isabella coloured and looked down.

"You won't try and do anything about it if I tell you?" she queried anxiously.

Valerie laughed.

"Don't know what you mean," she said.

"You won't make them have me if I'm not big enough?" Isabella blundered. "They said it would spoil the look of the show, and so it would. But I thought—if I *could* grow—I might be big enough after all."

"What on earth are you talking about?"

"The Guide display. You won't make them have me if they don't want to?"

"I won't do anything. Now tell me about it."

So Isabella stumbled through the whole story, and Valerie listened in silence.

"D'you think I *have* grown?" she finished up.

Valerie grinned at her. But it was a friendly grin which did not hurt.

"No," she said decidedly, "I don't. You didn't really think you would, did you?"

And Isabella grinned back shyly.

"S'pose not," she allowed.

They stood for some minutes without speaking. Isabella was thinking that Valerie really was just as nice as she had always imagined, and that it was very wonderful and exciting to be talking to her like this. Then she relapsed into despair again. What was she to do for the Guides? She hadn't grown, and nobody wanted her.

It seemed that Valerie had read her thought, for she turned to her and spoke so suddenly that Isabella jumped.

"Look here," she said irritably, "why don't you do something that you *can* do? You'll never be any good at gym or games."

Isabella blushed with shame. Why, those were the only things it was any use being good at. But Valerie was going on—

"I know you think I'm cruel to say that. I'm not. It's true, and it's just silly for you to worry about it. You'd much better use up your time over things you can be good at, and get better at them."

"I don't think," Isabella ventured miserably, "that I'm good at anything."

"Rubbish!" Valerie snapped. "Everybody's good at something. Else, what 'ud be the use of them? What I was really thinking of, though," she went on, "was this. Aren't you always drawing, or writing, or something?"

Isabella went quite purple at that. Fancy Valerie knowing about her silly habits.

"I—I just write down—oh, things that happen!" she stammered. "I don't think they're any use."

"I've got an uncle," Valerie told her, "who publishes things. You write a story and I'll get him to look at it. He looks at my essays sometimes, but he says they're never any good. You might make heaps more for the Guides that way than helping at a silly old gym display. People make lots of money by writing."

"What should I write about?" Isabella asked doubtfully.

"Something you know about. School, I should think."

"I'll try. I'll really try. Do you think I could do it?"

"Don't see why not. Get along out of the gym now into the garden."

Isabella perceived that Valerie was a prefect again, and vanished discreetly.

Round and round the garden she strolled, with eyes for nobody, full of her own hurrying thoughts. Valerie thought she could write. Valerie thought she might be of some use. Valerie was going to help her.

After prep she raced home and scribbled and scribbled. She was furious when bedtime came. She had had no idea that it would take so long to write a story. But it was tremendous fun, and awfully easy once you had started.

On the third day she lay in wait for Valerie.

"I've finished it!" she announced.

Valerie had not forgotten. She smiled in most friendly fashion.

"Good work. My uncle wants to see you. I'll give you his address." She scrabbled in her pocket for paper and pencil. "Here. Can you go round after school this afternoon? It's quite close."

• • • • • • •

After that, events moved with astonishing speed. First there was an interview with a fat, kind man with wrinkles round his eyes, who took possession of her story and said he would read it and let her know what he thought of it. Then the next day Valerie, twinkling mysteriously, actually waited for her, and said that the uncle wanted to see her again and took her to his house. The fat man laughed at her and called her a talented young lady, and made her simply gasp by presenting her with four crackly pound notes and four shillings.

"Four guineas," he said. "I think that's fair. It'll come out in next month's *Schoolgirl*. D'you read the *Schoolgirl*? Yes?

That's right. Look out for it. And if you can do me three more as good as this, I'll give you the same for each of them."

"That," said Valerie as they went out, "is sixteen guineas right off. And he told me he'd take as many more as you could do. Look here, my people want to know you. I told them you weren't a bad kid. Will you come to tea on Saturday?"

'The Reformers' appeared in The Great Book for Girls, *Oxford University Press, 1934.*

"I SAY, Tiddliwinks has put a new kid into our room!"

"What a *blight*! … What's its name, anyway?"

"Fay Harrison! I saw it on the list."

"Poor little reptile … 'spose she's fat, with a name like that!"

Giggles. Then, "Well, it *is* a blight. We shall have to set a Good Example and all that. I say, do you think that's her? Well, she *isn't* fat, but look at her *hair*!"

Joan and Pamela were strolling in the garden on the first day of term. Pamela had arrived early and tidied herself and prowled about, and Joan, having rushed upstairs to take off her outdoor clothes, had come down at once to join her. Last year, their dormitory had been a collection of kindred spirits who had enjoyed life very thoroughly, while just keeping on the right side of authority. This term, one of them had left, and the "new kid," to their annoyance, was her successor.

They watched the matron take charge of her and show her the way upstairs, and in a minute saw her peeping out of an upstair window.

"Yes, there she is—oh, well—she looks meek enough; I expect we'll be able to lick her into shape! I wonder if she can make those sausages herself?"

By the time tea was over the new girl's hair was the gossip of the junior school. Every one else had some sort of bob or crop, or—a few of them—a discreet pigtail. But over Fay Harrison's shoulders and almost to her waist there fell a cascade of pale gold ringlets, each one sleek and tidy, all perfectly parallel except for one extra fat one which escaped over each shoulder.

Joan whispered, "I wonder if there'll be soup for supper?"

"Idiot—why?"

"Because those sausages'll get into it if she isn't careful!"

There was not, so they had no chance of seeing what would have happened. But at bedtime the sausages caused some more amusement; for when all the rest of them were battering at their heads with the short hairbrushes, handle-less, which they affected, the matron marched in, beckoned to the new girl and marched out again, and in a few minutes Fay came back alone—with every one of the ringlets done up separately in a piece of white rag!

The dormitory was convulsed. Never having witnessed their great-aunts preparing for bed, none of them had ever seen anything like it before. They besieged her—"I say, can you sleep on all those bumps?"

She replied quite solemnly that the curl-rags were soft and did not get in her way at all.

"Don't you hate the beastly things?" one of them asked.

Fay looked positively reproving. "My mother's very proud of my beautiful hair," she said. "I have to take care of it."

They gave up teasing her for that night, then. There must be something wrong with a person who, at eleven, could think hair was worth being uncomfortable for.

Even during the day they found her difficult to tease. She kept the same air of rather disdainful aloofness towards them all; she did not seem to want them to talk to her, yet was not in the least afraid of them. She was very good at her work, and would not play rounders or hockey or anything because, she said, she did not like rough games. She had her bed moved away from the door (where new girls' beds always went because it was the nastiest place in the room) on the plea that the draught from it might give her rheumatism. She would not go into the swimming-bath for the same reason. She always took the biggest piece of cake at tea, and so much jam that there was hardly enough for the others. "If she didn't she'd get thin, I suppose," Joan sniffed.

In fact, she did all the things which every one thought of as simply awful, as if they were the most perfectly proper way for her to behave.

One day at tea the rest of them, on purpose, emptied the jam-dish between them before it reached her, and she simply got up and rang the bell for some more, and smiled so sweetly on the maid that it came with no protest at all.

And every night and every morning she vanished into the room of Tiddliwinks the matron (because she wore a row of coloured buttons down the front of her uniform and another down the back), and came out with her sausages twisted up or beautifully fat and polished according to the time of day.

Pamela tried to get a rise out of her by offering one night to undress her. But all Fay did was to say solemnly, "Thank you, you might undo my petticoat," and, when she had done so, handed her the garment to fold up with the words, "It goes in the left-hand corner of my middle drawer, and you might bring my bedsocks while you're there!"

"Just as if I were the miserable creature's lady's maid!" Pamela snorted in enormous indignation.

Then one morning at break there was the most alarming hullabaloo all of a sudden. Someone shrieked, "Oh, I've cut my finger off! I've cut my finger off! Oh, oh, oh, send someone for the doctor!"

There was such a tornado of yells that half the school rushed indoors to fetch Tiddliwinks, and the other half dashed in the direction of the sound. And there, of course, they found Fay, prostrate on the grass, bellowing, with her mouth wide open, only shutting it when it was necessary to take a breath and then for as short a time as possible. She was holding one hand in the other and wringing them both, and the handkerchief which was round them was spotted with blood.

Pamela approached her with curiosity. "Cut your finger off? How?"

"O-o-o-h, with my pocket-knife—o-o-o-h!" Fay lamented, rocking up and down.

"Where's the finger?" was Pamela's next question. She wondered whether it was possible to sew a finger on again.

Fay stopped howling and looked at her with scorn. "Here, of course," she said, and held it up; bleeding, certainly, quite a bit, but whole except for a small cut near the tip.

"But I thought you said you'd cut it off!" Pamela's tone was one of acute disappointment.

"So I have, p—p—practically!" Fay wrapped the hand up again jealously and began to moan and rock herself about. "O-o-o-oh, isn't the doctor coming? I shall bleed to death, o-o-oh!"

Pamela said sternly, "Stop it, you silly baby! Making all that fuss for a little cut!"

But Fay only blubbered that it wasn't a little cut, it was a great big frightful one, and nothing would stop her sobs.

The matron arrived with iodine and bandages. Fay's yells when she felt the sting of the iodine must have been audible for miles. All those who were near her simply had to clap their hands over their ears or risk being deafened. Tiddliwinks' comforting, "Now, count ten, and by the time you've done it will have stopped hurting!" had no effect at all.

The hand was bandaged and Fay, supported, was led into the house, still sobbing noisily. She did not appear again that day. Tiddliwinks, when the girls asked about her, said, "She's terribly weak, poor little thing! Such a shock to the system!"

Pamela snorted, "Shock to my eye! I've never heard such a fuss about nothing in all my life!" as soon as the matron was out of hearing.

Joan said seriously, "You know, I think something ought to be done about that kid. She's been here long enough now to realise that people here simply *don't* behave like that. And yet she goes on getting worse and worse. To-day's simply the limit. She's a disgrace to the dormitory and the form and the school itself."

"Hear, hear!" Pamela agreed, "and again, hear, hear! But I can't imagine what *can* be done. Hints aren't any good; they simply don't go through her hide."

"She's so perfectly certain that everything she does must be right that—that she can't imagine it might not be!"

"And the way she assumes that everybody's here just to do things for *her* is too sickening!"

"It's an awful pity Tiddliwinks plays up to her. I believe she *likes* messing about with that frightful hair!"

"Anyway," Pamela said, "what are we going to do?"

Joan said, "I've got several ideas. They've been maturing for the last few days. It all depends which we get a chance to do first."

The next morning Fay came down with her arm in a sling and an expression as of one about to burst into tears. She did dissolve once when the maths. mistress spoke a little sharply to her, and sniffed quietly for the rest of the lesson. When the form had to move to another room for a class she waited for the girl next to her to carry her books, and murmured pathetic thanks when she did. At drill, she fell out and protested that she was too weak even to march, and the gym. mistress smiled on her and said, “Yes, dear—yes, of course!”

“Just because she’s got curls—home-made ones—and a cut a quarter of an inch long! I’d be ashamed!” Pamela whispered, and was given a disorder mark for talking.

At break Pamela was in such a rage that she dashed away to the farthest corner of the garden, with Joan behind her. “I won’t stay where I can even see the wretched little rabbit!” she grumbled, and was in such a hurry that she tripped over a root and barked her shin against the trunk of a tree. She surveyed the damage gloomily. “Boo-hoo-hoo, it’s bleeding!” she announced crossly. “I’ve knocked off my leg, I’ve knocked off my leg! What are you *laughing* at, you blithering idiot? Nobody laughed at Fay!”

“This,” Joan announced, “is where we can do one of my ideas! I meant to do it myself, but this is too good to waste. D’you think you could make it bleed a little more?”

“It might, if I squeezed it,” Pamela said cautiously, and tried, without much success.

“A paint-box, I think,” said Joan. “Can you get back to the house? Or—no, perhaps we’d better do it here, it’s more private. You sit still till I come back.”

She was back in a very short time with a paintbox and a bottle of water. She squatted down and mixed colours busily, and as she mixed she talked. When she had finished, Pamela said resignedly, “You can do anything you like as long as you don’t poison my leg!”

“I shan’t do that. If only you can make it bleed a bit more I shan’t have to put any paint near the graze. Stamp about and see if that’ll do it!”

Chuckling, Pamela stamped; and produced a thin trickle from her wound which ran down her leg and pleased Joan exceedingly.

"That's topping! Do you think this is quite the right red? That's better! Now let's try!"

Painting was one of the things Joan was good at. She adorned the lower part of Pamela's leg to such effect that it looked as though it had been involved in a motor accident. A realistic mixture of vermilion and crimson-lake streamed down from a splodge just below the knee, where a liberal application of black and green gave the illusion of a bruise. A red puddle lodged between the white sports sock and Pamela's ankle, and soaked gradually into the sock ("It'll wash out, I expect," Joan said, "and anyway, it's in a good cause." Pamela said, "I can always have them dyed"). As a final touch, a big handkerchief which Joan had brought out with her was daubed with the red mixture and tied on, clean side inwards, so that only the edge of the original very small graze could be seen.

Joan stowed the paintbox away in its satchel, which might have held books or anything, and looked at her work with pride. "It 'ud take in even a doctor, I believe," she declared. "Come on now, lean on me and look most extraordinarily brave. We'll have to go rather a long way round, because our prey is parked down by the tennis court. Ready? Hop!"

"I needn't hop *yet*!" Pamela protested, and scuttled along the path till the tennis court was almost in sight. "*Now* let's begin!"

Slowly, painfully, but with evident stoic determination, she limped on Joan's arm towards Fay, who was lying gracefully on the grass bank with a book. They had nearly reached her when Joan said loudly, "Look here—I really don't think you ought to go any farther! I'll leave you here and go and fetch Tiddles!"

Pamela sighed. "I—can go on!" she gasped in a little weak voice. "Let me—go on! I don't—want to trouble—Tiddliwinks to come—out!"

"Well, well, just let's rest," said Joan compassionately. "Then you can go on again in a minute." She deposited her burden skilfully on the grass at Fay's side.

Pamela looked up sickly and whispered, "Oh, it's you!" and saw Fay's eyes, horror-stricken, fixed upon her leg before she collapsed.

"How awful! How simply awful! What ever have you done?" Fay gasped.

Pamela seemed to pull herself together. She sat up and looked about her, sticking the leg out straight in front. "That?" she looked at it carelessly. "Oh, that's only a graze. Caught it on a twig in the wood."

Fay squatted beside it, fascinated. Her own arm was still in its sling.

"A graze? But it's terrible! Is it all—blood?"

Pamela raised her eyebrows. "What else could it be?" she inquired. "Nothing to make a flap about!" She got to her feet, not without several agonised twitchings of the face, which she controlled at once. "Arm, please, Joan. I'm all right now. I just felt stupidly faint, but it's gone off with the rest."

Fay's eyes were like saucers. "Aren't you brave!" she said in an admiring whisper. "I can't let you go all the way like that! I'll dash in and fetch Matron out—she'd be furious if you went all the way, I'm sure!" She was gone before they could stop her.

The conspirators looked at each other in dismay. "You said it would take in even a doctor!" Pamela murmured. "Shall we risk it? Or hide?"

Joan glanced towards the garden door. Tiddliwinks was already coming at full speed. "Risk it!" she grinned. "Come on, sit down again!"

They need not have worried. Tiddliwinks was not suspicious by nature, and she loved attending to wounds. She threw one look at the leg and went into action. "No business to be walking on that, none at all!" she said. "Joan, help me to give her a dandy-chair! That's right! Comfortable? Fay, you go in front and open the doors!"

She went through all the paraphernalia of clean water, iodine, and bandage. She did say doubtfully once, "It's a very small place to have bled so much!" but Pamela disarmed her by agreeing cheerfully, "It's an idiotic little place! But I always do bleed pints when I cut myself!"

"Well, I'm sure you must feel very weak after losing all that. You'd better stay where you are till tea-time, anyway. Is there any one you'd like to come and see you?"

"Joan, please. And Fay Harrison," Pamela decided.

Fay was still bleating about Pamela's bravery when they came

She threw one look at the leg and went into action.

in. Joan took the opportunity of fixing her with an accusing eye, and saying firmly, "That's how people do behave when they hurt themselves at this school. We came that long way round, in spite of all the pain Pamela was in, specially to show you. D'you see?"

Fay's fair face flushed scarlet and paled again. "D'you mean—you think *I* didn't behave properly—about this?" She was quick enough at the uptake.

"That's exactly what we do mean!" Joan told her severely. "I saw you there when I ran in to get—the—the dressings—and we thought we couldn't miss the opportunity of letting you see how people *do* take—hurts—here. And, while we're at it, of telling you that we simply loathe any one who cares whether she's comfortable or not—whether she sits in a draught—and whether she looks pretty—and who can't look after herself and do her own hair and fold up her own clothes, and take the smallest bit of cake and the littlest helping of jam just because she's a new kid and ought to know her place. You may be a little tin goddess at home—but here you're—just a worm—see?"

Fay was looking more and more puzzled as the oration went on.

"D'you mean—*I* ought to do those things?" she demanded.

Joan was exasperated. "What d'you think I mean, if not that?"

Fay's lips trembled. Then, surprisingly, she squared her shoulders and controlled herself. "I—never thought of things—that way. I—never have done things for myself—and I've never really hurt myself before, and I was terrified!"

Joan and Pamela stared at her. There was something about her which, in spite of themselves, they liked. They had expected her to rage or to burst into tears.

She was looking at Pamela almost with awe. "I've never

thought of any one being as brave as you are!" she said. "I'll never make a fuss about a cut again as long as I live!"

She stole away, leaving Pamela and Joan staring after her in comic dismay. Pamela mumbled, "Oh, blow! I do feel such a pig!"

It was at that minute that Tiddliwinks burst in like a whirlwind, carrying in her hand a dripping, pinkish handkerchief. "You little monkeys—what d'you mean by it? Is there anything wrong with your miserable leg at all, or is it *all* paint?" she demanded. "Telling me a whole string of whackers!"

Pamela became dignified. "We didn't tell you a single, solitary one! I did graze my leg on a tree-trunk, and it did bleed—about two spots! You look!" She pulled off the bandage and stuck the leg out for inspection.

The matron sniffed. She said inconsequently, "Poor little Fay's mother's right away in India. It's not fair to be hard on her."

Joan said firmly, "My mother's right away in Scotland, and I don't see her in term any more than Fay sees hers. I don't see that's any reason for being soft … if her father's a soldier she jolly well ought to be braver than we are!"

Pamela giggled reminiscently. "She says she's never going to make a fuss about anything again after seeing me be so brave," she said. "It was only an object-lesson, and we didn't really mean to bring you into it at all, only she went off and fetched you. *Now* are you going to spoil it all by telling her it was nothing but paint?"

The matron looked from one to the other of them and shut her mouth up with a snap. "On second thoughts, I am not. But," she glared at Pamela, "you jolly well get up off that bed, my child, and go down to tea, bandage and all!"

Fay went about for the next few days more solemnly than ever. She discarded her sling, she did not ask any one to do a single thing for her, she only took the veriest scraping of jam, and hardly any cake. And she insisted on sharpening Pamela's pencils for her and doing any little odd jobs she could find. When she came back after the half-term holiday her hair was brushed out into a wavy tail and tied back with a bow, and she carried a tennis racquet under her arm and a bathing-suit in her bag. She arrived early, and appropriated the bed which was nearest the door.

Pamela, seeing her, exclaimed, "What the dickens!" and stared.

Fay, with a twinkle in her eye, which warmed Pamela's hard heart, said, "I've decided to stop being an infant in arms and turn into a schoolgirl, that's all. You've no idea what a fight it's been with the aunt I'm living with!"

She and Joan and Pamela became an inseparable trio before the term was over. And by the time they told her the truth about Pamela's wounded leg she knew them well enough to laugh and declare that she had very well deserved it.

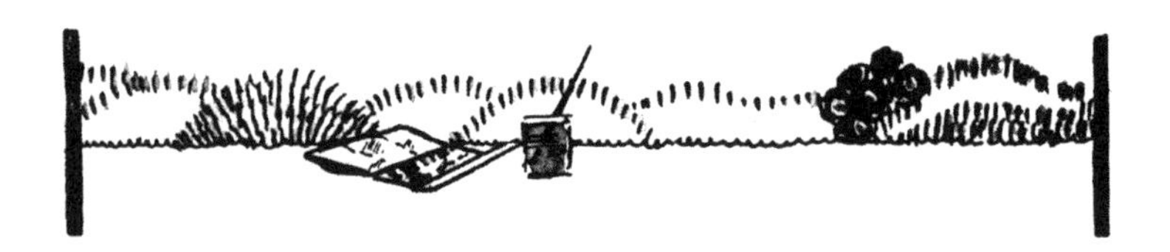

Girls Gone By Publishers

Girls Gone By Publishers republish some of the most popular children's fiction from the 20th century, concentrating on those titles which are most sought after and difficult to find on the second-hand market. Our aim is to make them available at affordable prices, and to make ownership possible not only for existing collectors but also for new collectors so that the books continue to survive. We also publish some new titles which fit into this genre.

Authors on the GGBP fiction list include Angela Brazil, Margaret Biggs, Elinor Brent-Dyer, Dorita Fairlie Bruce, Patricia Caldwell, Gwendoline Courtney, Winifred Darch, Monica Edwards, Josephine Elder, Antonia Forest, Lorna Hill, Clare Mallory, Dorothea Moore, Violet Needham, Elsie Jeanette Oxenham, Malcolm Saville and Evelyn Smith.

We also have a growing range of non-fiction titles, either more general works about the genre or books about particular authors. Our non-fiction subjects include Girl Guiding, Monica Edwards and her books, Elsie Oxenham's books, and Geoffrey Trease. These books are in a larger format than our fiction titles, and most of them are lavishly illustrated in colour as well as black and white.

For details of availability and when to order see our website—www.ggbp.co.uk—or write for a catalogue to GGBP, 4 Rock Terrace, Coleford, Radstock, BA3 5NF, UK.

Some of our books are available as eBooks. These are only available from our website, www.ggbp.co.uk